"I like what being with you does to me, Ana."

Rock shifted, tugged her closer.

"But you want to own me?"

"No." He stepped back, ran a hand through his hair. "I'm saying…you're the one, Ana. You're the one who's changing and reshaping me."

He felt her hand on his arm. "I don't want to change you. I just want to understand you."

Rock put his arms around her again, savoring the warmth of her skin, the sweetness of holding her. "I'm not explaining this right," he said. He urged her close, then lowered his mouth to hers.

The kiss held all of his dark secrets, all of his fears and worries. As his lips moved over hers, he felt those secrets and fears being shifted into something good and right, into something full of light and hope.

Books by Lenora Worth

Love Inspired

LENORA WORTH

grew up in a small Georgia town and decided in the fourth grade that she wanted to be a writer. But first she married her high school sweetheart, then moved to Atlanta, Georgia. Taking care of their baby daughter at home while her husband worked at night, Lenora discovered the world of romance novels and knew that's what she wanted to write. And so she began.

A few years later, the family settled in Shreveport, Louisiana, where Lenora continued to write while working as a marketing assistant. After the birth of her second child, a boy, she decided to pursue her dream full-time. In 1993, Lenora's hard work and determination finally paid off with that first sale.

"I never gave up, and I believe my faith in God helped get me through the rough times when I doubted myself," Lenora says. "Each time I start a new book, I say a prayer, asking God to give me the strength and direction to put the words to paper. That's why I'm so thrilled to be a part of Steeple Hill's Love Inspired line, where I can combine my faith in God with my love of romance. It's the best combination."

THE CARPENTER'S WIFE

LENORA WORTH

Love Inspired.

Published by Steeple Hill Books™

STEEPLE HILL BOOKS

Steeple
Hill

ISBN 0-373-87218-6

THE CARPENTER'S WIFE

Copyright © 2003 by Lenora H. Nazworth

Visit us at www.steeplehill.com

Printed in U.S.A.

In God is my salvation, and my glory;
the rock of my strength,
and my refuge....

—*Psalms* 62:7

To my nephew Chester Howell, with love

Chapter One

Rock Dempsey loved Sunset Island.

He loved the way the small island off the Georgia coast lay tossed like a woman's dainty slipper near the mainland. He loved the way the island sat at the mouth of the Savannah River, the land caught between a glistening oval-shaped bay and the ever-churning Atlantic Ocean. He loved having the sunrise to the east over the sea, and the sunset to the west over the bay.

As he stood in the middle of his workshop, with the ocean breezes coming through the thrown-open doors from the ocean on one side and the bay on the other, Rock decided a man couldn't ask for much more in life.

Unless that man was pushing thirty-five and his

whimsical mother was still asking him when he was going to settle down and produce a passel of grandchildren for her to spoil.

"Roderick, I could die and go to heaven without even a memory of a sweet baby to carry home with me," his mother, Eloise, had told him in a gentle huff just that morning when he'd stopped by for breakfast.

They had this same conversation at least once a week. It was never a good sign when his mother used his given name in a discussion. But then, his brothers Stone and Clay had to hear it from Eloise, too, each time they came to visit.

In her mid-fifties and long widowed, Eloise Dempsey kept close tabs on her three sons, properly named Roderick, Stanton and Clayton, but affectionately nicknamed Rock, Stone and Clay. She fretted that none of them had yet to make a lifetime commitment to one woman. If Rock blamed their artistic mother and her flighty ways for her sons' obvious fear of commitment, he'd never say that out loud to Eloise. She'd had enough heartache in her life, between being disinherited and then losing the man she had loved—and had given up that inheritance to be with—to the sea in a terrible storm. Even if she had sacrificed quality time with her sons to become one of the most famous sculpture artists in the South, Rock was trying very hard to come to terms with his lovable mother's flaws. And his own.

Rock reminded himself that Eloise was trying, now that she'd found success with her art, to make things up to her children. Still, the memories of eating TV dinners and going to bed tired after watching over his two younger brothers always left a bad taste in Rock's mouth.

Growing up, he'd often dreamed of a traditional family, with a mom and dad who were devoted to family and children, with good, home-cooked meals and nights spent together watching a movie or sharing a supper out on the shore. Rock and his brothers had missed out on those things. While their mother pursued her art, they had had to find odd jobs here and there to make ends meet. The islanders had been kind and watchful, and Eloise had continued her work, unaware and undisturbed, while her children had the run of the land.

If he closed his eyes, he could still hear the hiss of her welding torch, late into the night. The glare had always been too bright for Rock, but the sound of it never went away. If he looked north toward what the islanders called the Ankle Curve, he could just make out the turret of the rambling Victorian beach house where his mother had lived and worked for so many years. He could still see her there, in the big barn settled deep in the moss-covered trees that she used as a studio, bent over yet another bust shaped from clay or an aged cross forged from wood and stone. His mother's hands had created beauty.

But he'd missed those same hands tucking him in at night.

Not wanting to dwell on his mother's shortcomings—or his own in the love department, for that matter—Rock turned back to the cabinets he'd been restoring for Miss McPherson. Now, *there* was an available single woman. She was in church every Sunday, tithed regularly, cooked everything from Brunswick stew to clam chowder and had a smile that lit up a room. Too bad she was pushing eighty.

"One day I'm going to get up the courage to ask Miss Mac why she never married," Rock said to the gleaming oak cabinet door he'd just finished vanishing.

"Do you often talk to your cabinets?" a soft feminine voice said from the open shed doors.

Rock turned to find a petite, auburn-haired woman staring at him, her green eyes slanted and questioning, a slight smile on her angular face. He stood there like a big dummy while she walked into the quiet cool of his work shed, her crisp white cotton shirt and polished tan trousers giving her an air of sophistication.

Coming out of his fog, Rock grabbed a wipe rag and ran it over his hands. "I'm afraid I do tend to talk to my creations. A bad habit.'' Tossing the rag aside, he leaned back on the long, dented work table. ''What can I do for you?''

She pushed at a wave of burnished hair that kept falling over her chin. ''I'm Ana Hanson. I just moved into the Harper house—soon to be Ana's Tea Room and Art Gallery.''

''Oh.'' Trying to hide his surprise, Rock pushed off the table to extend a hand. ''My mother told me about you.''

And had urged him to get to know the *single* newcomer to the tiny island a little better. *''Ana will be lonely, Rock. Invite her to church, at least. Just as a way to break the ice.''*

''Well, don't look so glum,'' the woman said, her head tilting in defense. ''Did I come at a bad time?''

Despite his mother's very obvious suggestion echoing through his head, Rock tried to stick to the here and now. He felt horrible at the way he'd sounded. ''No, no. It's just—I had expected—I thought you'd be older, more like my Mother's other eccentric friends.'' Feeling more foolish with each word, he quickly added, ''Mom said you needed some new cabinets?''

Ana nodded through an amused smile, causing the same silky length of curls to fall right back across her face. ''Yes. As you probably know, the Harper house needed major renovations. Some of the preliminary work in the upstairs apartment has been done, thanks to my sister—she's a Realtor and has all kinds of connections with carpenters and contractors out of Savannah—but I wanted someone local and more accessible to help me renovate the kitchen and main dining area.''

"And that'd be me?" Rock grinned, glad that at least his mother's bragging often brought him new customers.

"You come highly recommended," Ana said as she ran a hand over a newly restored pie safe. "That's one reason I waited before finishing this part of the project. Your mother suggested we might work together on this—that you'd understand…what I expected…as far as cabinets and bookshelves go."

"That's just my mother talking," Rock responded, noting that the floral scent of Ana Hanson's perfume managed to find its way to his nose over the smell of sawdust and varnish stripper. "She thinks I inherited some of her artistic ability."

"I'd have to agree with Eloise," Ana replied, an appreciative expression on her face as her gaze moved over the many cabinets, armoires and chests Rock had either built from scratch or restored. "She seems to be a good judge of talent."

"How do you know my mother?" he asked, curious as to how Ana had found her way to Sunset Island.

"I worked at an art gallery in Savannah," Ana explained. "We exhibited some of your mother's work. I got to know her when we held a reception in her honor."

"Ah, that explains it, then," Rock said, turning to put away his tools. "My mother's reputation precedes all of us."

"You sound almost ambivalent about that."

He whirled to find Ana's luminous green eyes on him.

"It's a long story, but yes, I guess it still surprises me that she's so famous."

"She has a lot of talent."

"Yes, she does. I can't argue with that." He shrugged, brushed wood chips off the sleeve of his T-shirt. "Look, I love and respect my mother. And her designs are beautiful. But she works too hard— she's almost obsessed with it."

"Most good artists are that way, don't you think?"

Rock studied her for a minute, wondering if this cute woman was just like his mother. Would Ana Hanson put work above all else in her life? Probably, since she seemed anxious to make her tea room a success. "I guess you're right. And since you worked in an art gallery, you probably appreciate art more than I do. So why don't we stick to a subject I know best—cabinets. What do you have in mind?''

Ana had a lot of things in mind, but she didn't think Rock Dempsey wanted to hear about her hopes and dreams for this business venture. Should she tell him she'd had to sell practically everything she owned to make the down payment on the Harper house? Should she explain to him that, since college, her dream had been to own some sort of gallery? Should she go into detail about how her sister, Tara, had suggested Ana use her talent for cooking along with her good eye for art to come to Sunset Island and open a combination tea room and art gallery?

Ana watched as Rock busied himself with cleaning his workspace. He seemed on edge, resistant to her. Maybe because his mother had sent her to him. Did Rock think Eloise was up to more than just securing him another paying customer? Well, Ana could certainly nip that little concept right in the bud. She didn't have time for matchmaking, even if Eloise meant well.

Ana had to get her tea room ready for the grand opening in a few weeks. And that opening depended on how quickly Rock Dempsey could help her.

''I have several ideas,'' she said in answer to his earlier question. ''I want to build some cabinets and buffets in keeping with the Victorian flavor of the house. It was built around the turn of the last century.''

''I'm familiar with the history of the Harper house,'' he said, smiling. ''It's been vacant on and off over the years. When we were little, my brothers and I used to sneak in there at night, mostly to scare each other and see who would be the bravest by going into a dark, deserted house.''

Ana decided Rock Dempsey seemed the type to brave any situation. He was the standard tall, dark and handsome, with fire-flashing deep blue eyes. But his face had an interesting aged look that spoke of wisdom and gentleness, the same tanned richness of the priceless wooden furniture he worked hard to restore. Did Rock need a bit of restoration himself, maybe?

''So, who was the bravest?'' she asked.

He shrugged, grinned. ''Well, none of us was very brave. I think I managed to sneak in a back window once, but, of course, Stone and Clay decided to come around front and jiggle the door, shouting 'Police,' which naturally made me run away in terror—terror that my mother would ground me for life, rather than fear of authority.''

Ana started thumbing through a design book. ''Sounds as if you and your brothers had an exciting life growing up.''

''We had our moments,'' he said. ''We've always been close—or…we were growing up. I guess we've drifted apart lately, though.''

''That's too bad,'' Ana replied, thinking of the tenuous relationship she had with her sister Tara. Tara was hard to read at times, a type-A personality with a lightning temper and bitter memories. Ana harbored some of that same bitterness, directed toward her sister at times, toward herself at others. But she didn't want to think about that right now. She had to get back to work.

''So, anyway, I thought you might come by the house later today, if possible, to look at the kitchen and dining room. It's been completely overhauled—painted, new flooring, but I held off on the final plans. I want it to be perfect.''

Rock handed her several more design books. ''Okay, then. Why don't you glance over these— there are several Victorian reproductions and some original restoration projects in there—and I'll meet you at the house, say, around four?''

''That would be good. I have some errands to run, but I should be back in plenty of time.'' She extended a hand. ''Thanks…Rod—''

''It's Rock,'' he said, wincing. ''My mother's choice of given names for her sons has left us the laughingstock of the island, I'm afraid.''

''I like your name,'' Ana said, acutely aware of the strength and warmth of his big callused hand.

"Well, around here, everyone calls me Rock," he said. "Or...Preacher Rock."

Ana jerked her hand back. "You're a preacher?"

"Just on Sundays," he said, a teasing light making his dark eyes go as blue as the ocean at night. "I got the job by being in the right place at the wrong time, or something like that."

"You're going to have to explain."

He walked with her out into the oak-shadowed yard, then pointed to the tiny whitewashed church sitting like a child's playhouse a few yards away from his cottage and workshop. "Reverend Palczynski was the island preacher for over forty years. He lived in this cottage, preached every Sunday in the Sunset Chapel. Then one day he came out to the workshop to get his volleyball equipment—he loved to play volleyball—and fell over dead right underneath this great live oak. He was ninety."

"Oh, goodness."

"Yes, *goodness* is a perfect word for Reverend Pal—as we all called him. He was a good man. I happened to come along and find him. Tried to save him, but he was already gone by the time the paramedics got here. He died with a smile on his face, but his death left a great void on the island."

"And you filled that void?"

Rock nodded, glanced out to the beach in the

distance. The roar of the ocean ran through the delicate tropical breezes that moved around the palm trees and great oaks. "One of the paramedics suggested I take over, since I'd always helped out at the chapel, doing odd jobs around the place, building cabinets and such. And since I have a reputation for being a philosopher of sorts, word got out. The town gossip, Greta Epperson, wrote about it in her society column in the *Sunset Sentinel,* and next thing I knew I was standing before the church elders, being blessed as their next preacher."

Ana laughed. "Your mother warned me people on the island do things their own way."

"Yes, that's true. We march to the beat of a different drummer, I think. And Greta captures it all in her column each week."

"Do you regret being…coerced into becoming a preacher?"

"No, not at all. You see, I believe no one can make me do something I don't want to do in the first place. It seemed a natural transition, since I worked out here—I already rented this space from Reverend Pal, anyway."

"So you moved right on in?"

The look he gave her made Ana's heart lift like a surprise wave coming through still waters. His eyes were filled with a quiet determination and a firm challenge.

"I've been known to move right in on a situation, yes."

She whirled, headed to her car. "Then, I'm sure I can count on you to deliver my cabinets and shelves in a timely manner. I'd like to open by mid-May."

"You don't beat around the bush, do you," she heard him say from behind her.

She also heard the crunch of his workboots on the shell-scattered drive. "I don't have time to mess around," Ana explained as she opened her car door and tossed the design books on the seat. "This is my last chance."

"Last chance for what?"

He was right there beside her, holding the car door open.

Ana slid behind the wheel, then looked up at him through the open window. "My last chance to make it. I've wanted this for a very long time. I don't intend to blow it."

"Got a lot invested in this, huh?"

She nodded, tried to relax. "Yes, time, money, commitments to several artists, your mother included. I don't want to let anybody down."

He leaned in, his big body blocking out the sun's bright rays. Ana got a whiff of aftershave mixed with turpentine. And got nervous all over again— her heart was doing the wave thing in rapid succession now.

"Then, *I* won't let *you* down," he told her.

Ana waited a couple of beats before stammering, "Th-thank you. I'll see you at four."

He smiled, then slowly stood back from the car. "See you then."

As Ana drove away, she heard the echo of his words. *"I won't let you down."*

She'd heard that one before. Many times.

But this time, she prayed it was the truth.

"I know. Amassing his fortune."

"Don't be bitter, Rock."

"I'm not bitter. Stone has his life and I have mine. I'm content right here on the island."

Eloise pulled dead heads off a nearby pink begonia. "Stone was never content living on the island. Savannah suits him much better."

Rock took a long drink from the tea, the sweet mint taste going down smooth in spite of the turmoil he always felt when talk turned to his brother, Stone. "I'm sure it does. And we all want Stone to be happy."

"That's exactly what I want—for all my sons. At least Clay seems to be thriving with the police department in Atlanta."

"Clay has always been a happy-go-lucky, hard-working fellow."

"He has a good heart."

"I couldn't agree more. In fact, I think Clay got the heart that Stone never had."

Eloise gave him a mock glare. "Stone has a heart. He just doesn't like to show it. I only want all of you to…find love, the kind of love I had with your father."

Not wanting to get into a long discussion on that topic because talking about her late husband always seemed to upset Eloise, Rock said, "So is that why you're throwing me at your friend Ana Hanson?"

Eloise reached for a yellow watering pitcher sitting in the bay window over the sink. Outside, a seagull cawed noisily in a low fly-by. "Who said I was throwing you at her? I just suggested you'd be perfect to help design her tea room, is all."

Rock chuckled. "Mom, why didn't you tell me she was young and pretty...and apparently single?"

His mother gave an eloquent shrug, her dangling turquoise feathered earrings brushing against the crocheted lace of her cream-colored linen tunic. "I figured if I told you about Ana, you'd clam up like a crab in a sand hole and refuse the job."

"I never turn down paying customers."

"Even cute...*available* ones?"

"Okay, I might have been a little hesitant if I'd known Ana was close to my age and single. But I have to admit, she is very pretty." He finished off the tea. "She *is* single, right?"

"Very much so," Eloise replied, her smile widening to reveal an endearing gap between her front teeth. "So, is that or the fact that she is attractive, smart, capable and...*available* going to hinder your working for her?"

"Probably," he said. "But then, it might just make it interesting, too. As Auguste Renoir said, 'Why should beauty be suspect?'"

"That's the spirit," Eloise replied, clasping her hands together. "Well, then, if you don't want some fruit and yogurt for dessert, I'll go back to my own work.''

"I'm fine, Mom. Got to get moving.''

Eloise whirled by, giving him a quick peck on the cheek. "I'll see you later.''

Rock watched as his mother moved gracefully over the steps leading from the wraparound porch and walked down the path to what had once been a horse stable, her soft leather walking sandals making very little noise.

The gardens were in full bloom—the fuchsia bougainvillea, the rich red hibiscus trees, the crape myrtle and azaleas all splashing together like a bright abstract painting underneath the Spanish moss of the ancient oak trees. And his mother in her feathered turquoise jewelry and flowing broomstick skirt fit right into the picture. Beautiful.

That made him think again of Ana Hanson. His mother had left out one trait he thought he recognized in the petite auburn-haired dynamo—ambition. And he remembered another favorite quote from a long-dead philosopher: "Beauty and folly are generally companions.''

She'd come here for companionship. For the warm ocean breezes and wonderful, salty mist of the sea. She'd come here to put down roots and settle in like the sea oats that flowed in wheat-colored patterns down on the dunes.

"I'm going to be a success," Ana promised herself as she glanced around the large near-empty kitchen of her tea room. "I have to make this work."

"I think you're off to a good start," Jackie Welsh, her just-hired assistant said as she passed by and grabbed her purse off the counter. "I'll be here bright and early tomorrow to begin training Tina and the other servers."

"Thanks," Ana told the tall brunette. "I appreciate your help so much."

She'd hired Jackie a few days ago, and already they were able to read each other's minds. She'd need that kind of connection when things got to hopping around here.

Glancing at her watch, she mentally went over her to-do list while she waited for Rock Dempsey. The two-bedroom upstairs apartment was done. Everything was unpacked and in place, and the entire staff had been hired. Over the next month or so, they'd help set things up and learn the menus and recipes by heart. Next week, the furnishings for the shop and tea room would start arriving. She'd have plenty to keep her busy then. Especially if Rock was here every day, measuring and building.

Just thinking of his big, muscular frame in the middle of her dainty treasures made Ana smile. It felt good to smile. She'd been so focused on this venture over the past few months, she'd forgotten how to relax. But now, she was here at last. Here in her own place, with her own living quarters— no roommates, no rent to pay—just a big mortgage that her sister had helped finance—she had no one to answer to except herself. She'd finally accomplished her dream.

Now she had to make that dream work.

She envisioned the wicker bistro tables she'd found at a clearance sale sitting here and there in what once had been the parlor of the house. She saw intimate groupings out on the long porch, where diners would have a clear view of the glistening bay down the sloping yard to the dunes. She'd put some nice cushiony rocking chairs out there, too.

Glancing down at the big bay, Ana saw a sailboat glide by like a giant blue and white butterfly. Maybe she could go sailing herself soon. It had been a long time since she'd sailed out on the water with the sun on her face.

A knock at the stained-glass front door caused her to jump. Not one for woolgathering, Ana scooted across the room, her espadrilles barely making a click on the polished wooden floors. Adjusting her clothes and hair, she opened the door to find Rock standing there in jeans and a T-shirt emblazoned with Save the West Island Lighthouse Summer Jam Session.

"Hi," she said, smiling as she ignored the way her pulse seemed to quicken each time he looked at her. Then she pointed to the image of the old West Island Lighthouse on his shirt. "You, too, huh? Eloise told me several islanders are working to renovate the lighthouse. And I read about the jam session in that Greta woman's column. That should be a challenge, from what I hear—raising funds for renovation."

He entered the room, ran his gaze over the pale cream painted walls and the feminine wallpaper border that depicted shoes, hats and purses from the turn of the century. Then he turned to her.

"I like a good challenge."

"Well, then, you'll love the job I have for you," she replied, her nerves stretching as tight as the rigging on a sail. "I hope…I think I have everything in order." With a wave of her hand, she strolled around the empty rooms. "As you can see, the walls and floors are done. And I've ordered some armoires and side-buffets for displays. They should be here any day now. The major appliances are all brand-new and industrial size—those will be installed this week. Mainly, I need you to take a look at the kitchen cabinets and tell me if they can be salvaged. And I'd like you to maybe redo the walk-in pantry and build some functional shelves in the kitchen, too."

Rock stood listening, his gaze once again moving over the central hallway and two long open rooms on each side of the front of the house. "The original parlor and dining room—this will be the restaurant area?"

"Yes, diners will be seated in both rooms, but our artwork and other wares will be displayed on the walls and all around the dining tables. Then we have a room in the back for private parties, which will also display a collection of antiques and art. The cash register will be here in the vestibule by the front door. I found an antique counter in an old drugstore in Savannah. It's being shipped." She pointed to an open door off the rear of the hallway. "And I have a small office right across from the kitchen. There's a bathroom back there, too."

He nodded, made notes on a small pad. "You seem to like the Victorian era."

"I do," she said, grinning. "I've always loved old things, all periods of history. Maybe because I read a lot growing up—stories of long ago, all about valor and romance."

"Oh?" He stopped writing and glanced up at her. "I'd figure you'd have been too busy chasing off boys who wanted their own valor and romance, to sit around reading books."

Blushing, Ana shook her head. "My sister got all the boys. I got my romantic *ideas* from books."

He stopped scribbling to stare at her. "I reckon

you do look like a Jane Austen kind of girl—all *Sense and Sensibility*."

Unsure if that was a compliment, Ana replied, "I'm a little old-fashioned and sensible, but I try not to live in the past."

"'The tender grace of a day that is dead…will never come back to me.'"

Stunned, Ana shrugged. It was as if Rock had hit on her deepest, most bittersweet memories with the precision of cupid's arrow. "That's…very melancholy."

"Alfred, Lord Tennyson," Rock explained. "This house has a tender grace. Maybe it will bring you a little romance…and some comfort."

Comfort? Was that what she'd been seeking all her life? Ana pushed at the dark memories blocking out the rays of hope in her mind. "Romance I doubt. But I guess I could use some comfort. Anyway, I love this house. And I'm thrilled to be here on the island. We used to vacation here with my parents. I fell in love with Sunset Island and I've always wanted to come back."

"You came from Savannah?"

"Yes. We lived out from Savannah, near Fort Stewart. My parents still live there in a house on the Canoochee River. Tara—that's my sister—and I attended college at Savannah State." She stopped, took a breath. "I was a senior when she was a freshman. She got married a year later and never finished college. After I graduated, I moved to Savannah to work in the art gallery." She lowered her eyes, stared at an aged spot in the floor, memories as rich as the lacquer on the wood coloring her mind. "Anyway, now I'm here. I'm moving forward, even if I do like things from the past."

Ana quieted, thinking she sounded as if she were trying to convince herself of this. And maybe she was. She still had hurtful memories from her college days, memories that had colored her whole adult life and her rocky relationship with her younger sister. But she was determined to make a new start, with both her life and her sister.

"The past can be good," Rock said, his keen eyes sweeping over her face. "As long as we keep it in perspective."

"Oh, I keep it in perspective, all right. I don't want to ever go back there."

"Bad memories?"

Ana looked up at him, saw the sincere curiosity in his beautiful eyes. "Some." *Lots.* But she wasn't about to tell him any of that. She ruffled her hair with her hand. "Do you want to see the kitchen?"

"Sure."

She started toward the back of the house, heard him behind her, then willed her heart and her head to stay calm. Ana reminded herself that she'd given her heart to a man once, only to have it returned bruised and battered.

She would never make that mistake again. Even if this handsome preacher named Rock did cause her to think of romantic things like strolling on the beach at sunset and intimate dinners by candlelight.

Ana would stick to her art, her cooking and her books. Those were safe, tangible things.

Love wasn't safe. That "tender grace," as Rock had quoted, would never come back to her again. She was all business now. And all on her own.

If only Rock Dempsey's eyes would stop looking at her with that anything-but-business gaze.

This woman meant business.

Rock had measured, suggested, tested, rearranged, gauged and decided on what could be done for the beautiful old cabinets in the long, sunny kitchen. A good stripping of old paint, some new hardware and a lot of wood restorer and varnish would make them shine like new. That part had been easy.

But testing and gauging Ana Hanson—ah, therein lay the challenge of this assignment.

She had been hurt somewhere in the past. Maybe during her childhood, maybe during her college years. But something had left her unsure and unsteady, even if she did try to present a calm, capable facade to the world.

Rock had no doubt she was capable. She seemed as intent on making her tea room a popular tourist attraction as his mother did on creating intriguing artifacts from rocks and stones. That ability to focus should serve as a warning to Rock. Ana held many of the traits he'd seen too many times in his mother—that tendency to shut everything out, that need to finish the work, create the next sculpture piece, or, in Ana's case, create a haven for fine art and good food.

There was nothing wrong with that. But Rock wondered if Ana was pouring all of her strength into this new venture because she was running from the past. Running from herself, just as his mother had done most of her life.

Turning to see where she'd flittered off to this time, Rock found Ana standing on a footstool wiping one of the big bay windows in the front parlor. He almost called out to her, but then the way the last of the sun's rays were gleaming all around her from the open west window on the other side of the room caused him to stop and just watch.

She stood in the soft wind, her dark red hair shining in the soft afternoon sun. Her skin was glistening with a golden creaminess. She'd changed clothes since this morning and now her long floral skirt moved around her like a flower garden.

Rock took this picture in, and realized it had been way too long since he'd been out on a date with a pretty woman. And taking old Miss Mc-Pherson to the seafood market once a week didn't count.

"You hungry?" he heard himself saying.

Ana turned, almost too fast. She nearly fell off the stepstool. Rock wasn't fast enough to catch her, and he was glad. That would have been a classic romantic way of getting her into his arms—too obvious.

But since he didn't want to look unchivalrous, he did step forward. "Steady there."

"I'm fine," Ana said, stepping down from the stool to turn and stare at him as she pushed her hair away from her eyes. "I must have misunderstood you, though. I thought you asked me if I was hungry."

"No misunderstanding. I did—ask you that, I mean."

She stood there with her hands on her hips, an almost doubting glare on her pretty face. "Why did you—ask?"

So she was the suspicious type. "No particular reason, other than it's getting dark and…I only had a sandwich for lunch. I was thinking about fried catfish out at the Sunken Pier. Ever been there?"

"No."

"No, you've never been there, or no, you aren't hungry, or just plain 'no, I don't want to have dinner with you, Rock'?"

"No to the first, yes to the second, and…I'm not sure to the last part."

He crossed his hands over his chest, his trusty pocket notepad clutched in one hand. Then he leaned forward, offering up what he hoped was his best smile. "Why aren't you sure? It's just a meal. We can go over the cabinet plans again."

She frowned, looked around. "I guess we do need to finalize everything—set your hours, your fee, things like that."

"Exactly. A business dinner."

"Strictly business."

"Wouldn't dream of having it any other way."

He liked the trace of disappointment that had scurried through her green eyes. But he wouldn't dare tell her that since she'd walked into his shop this morning, he had at least thought of having things another way—besides the strictly business way, that is.

"I'll freshen up and get my purse," she said, clearly as confused and unsure as she'd been two minutes ago. "We won't be late, will we? I have so much paperwork—contracts with food vendors, inventory sheets to check over—"

"I'll have you home at a reasonable hour, I promise."

"Okay, then."

"Okay, then."

"You know, Mark Twain said principles have no real force except when one is well fed."

She rewarded him with a smile. "And you are clearly a man of principle."

"That I am. And manners. My mama taught me both."

"That I can believe," she said, her expression softening. "I trust your mother's opinion and her good judgment of character, even if you are her son and she has to recommend you on that basis alone. I think I'll be safe with you."

"Completely."

But as Rock watched her hurry up the narrow staircase, he had to wonder how much *he* could trust his mother's judgment. After all, Eloise had brought Ana and him together for her own maternal reasons.

And now Rock was worried about those reasons and about how being with this shy, old-fashioned woman made him feel.

The real question was—would *he* be safe with Ana Hanson?

Chapter Three

"And that's how it got its name," Rock said, waving a hand in the air toward the old partially sunken pier just outside the wide window.

Ana watched as he smiled, but the smile didn't quite reach his eyes. They held that distant darkness that seemed to flare like thunderclouds now and then. He looked down at his plate, then shrugged. "There's a lot of history on this old island."

Ana laughed, then nibbled the remains of her baked trout. "So you're telling me that pier used to be completely safe and sturdy, until twenty years ago when a hurricane came through and almost swept it into the sea? And because of that and the restaurant's legendary name, no one wants to fix the pier now?"

Rock nodded, grabbed a crispy hush puppy, then chewed before answering. ''The first restaurant got washed into the ocean. That was the original Seafood at the Pier fine dining establishment. It had been here since 1910. But after the hurricane, the only thing left was that part of the pier that's sticking up from the water now. A good place for pelicans and egrets to perch. The owner's son decided to rebuild under a new name—thus The Sunken Pier Restaurant. Been here and been going strong ever since, through storms and summer tourists alike, frying up fish and steaming up shrimp and lobster, oysters and clams—whatever bounty the sea has to offer.''

Ana stared out the window at the ocean. Dusk had descended over the water in a rainbow of pastel hues—some pinks and reds here, and a few mauves and blues there. The water washed against the ancient remains of the old pier, slapping against the aged wood pilings in an ever-changing, but never-ending melody of life. And what was left of the pier looked somehow symbolic of that life. The thick beams and timbers lay at a haphazard angle, crossways and sideways, like a pile of kindling, stopped in time in mid-collapse.

Ana thought that her own life seemed like that— at times she felt about to fall apart at any minute, but at other times, she dug in, refusing to give up in spite of being beaten down at every turn.

She looked back over at Rock. "I guess I can understand why they left it that way. It's a reminder of sorts."

"Exactly," he said, bobbing his head, a bittersweet smile crinkling his dark-skinned face. "My mother even did a sculpture based on that pier. She called it *The Resurrection* because the crossbeams of some of the pilings made her think of a cross. She made it out of wood and iron, with a waterfall flowing through it to represent the ocean and life."

"Where is this sculpture now?" Ana asked. "I imagine some collector snatched it up right away, but I don't recall seeing it in any of the trade catalogues or art books."

Rock's eyes darkened again and the smile disappeared from his face. "You probably never saw it because it wasn't for sale. But someone *acquired* the piece, anyway, many years after she'd finished it. Locked it away in a garden behind his fancy mansion up on the bluffs."

Sensing that Rock didn't approve of this particular art collector, Ana leaned forward. "Isn't that a good thing? That your mother sold the piece, I mean?"

He lifted his chin. "Normally, yeah, that's good, selling a fine piece of art. But she didn't get a very good price for what she had to give up."

And that's all he said. Wondering why he insisted on talking in riddles, Ana watched as he took a long swallow of his iced tea. "Rock," she said, "did I ask the wrong question?"

Rock glanced over at her as if he'd forgotten she was even there. "No, nothing like that. Let's change the subject."

Ana again got the impression that Rock somehow resented his mother's art. Maybe because it had taken his mother away from him and his brothers? It was a known fact in local art circles that Eloise Dempsey was a woman driven by her talent, a woman who had worked long and hard to become a successful force in the art world. It was also known, from various interviews and articles written about Eloise, that her relationship with her three grown sons was difficult. And even though Eloise knew exactly what to say in order to protect her privacy, she still managed, when necessary, to get a good sound bite on the evening news.

Deciding to venture forth, Ana said, "You know, Rock, I've read articles in the trade magazines about your mother. Being an artist is never easy. The art demands a lot, but you and Eloise seem so close. She brags on you—on all of her sons—and she did recommend you to me."

Rock held his tea glass in one hand while he watched the waves crashing against the seawall and pier outside. "We've managed to stay on good terms over the years, in spite of what the media might say. And in spite of what the world doesn't know or see."

Thinking he wasn't going to elaborate, Ana could only nod and sit silently. She didn't want to appear nosy, yet she yearned to understand what had brought that darkness to his beautiful eyes. "It must have been hard on all of you, losing your father when you were so young."

"It was tough," Rock finally said. "For a long time, we didn't understand why he had to die out there doing what he loved best, shrimping." He glanced out at the water again. "But then 'deep calleth unto deep' or so the scripture says."

"Did he die in a storm?"

"Yes." Rock nodded toward the toppled pilings. "The very same hurricane that took that pier."

Ana let out a little gasp that caused him to look across the space between them. "I'm sorry, Rock. Is that why you don't want to talk about the sculpture?"

He sighed, kept staring at her, his eyes now as dark and unreadable as the faraway waters over the distant horizon. "It's not the sculpture, Ana. It's the fact that my mother designed it out of grief and sorrow and made it into a beautiful symbol of redeeming love. She didn't sell the sculpture. She gave it to...someone who doesn't really appreciate it."

"Can you tell me who?"

Rock set his glass on the table, then folded his hands together across the white linen tablecloth. "I can tell you exactly who, and exactly why. My mother gave that sculpture to my brother Stone. And she gave it to him as a way of asking his forgiveness. Stone took the sculpture, but he has yet to forgive my mother…or me."

Ana had many more questions, but decided they had to wait. She wouldn't press Rock into talking about his obviously strained relationship with his middle brother, Stone. From what Ana knew, each of the three Dempsey brothers was successful in his own right. But Stone Dempsey was probably the most successful, business- and money-wise. She'd read somewhere a few years ago that Stone had bought Hidden Hill, a big stucco and stone turn-of-the-century mansion sitting atop the highest bluff on the island, not far from the West Island Lighthouse. But the mansion was crumbling around its foundations, from what Ana had heard. Which meant Stone had to have a lot of money to pour into restoration and renovations, at least.

Did Rock resent his brother's success?

As they strolled along the shoreline heading back to Rock's car, Ana couldn't picture this quiet, talented man resenting anyone because of money. Rock seemed content enough. He had a lovely cot-

tage near the Ankle Curve and he had his little
church. He had his own talent, too. His cabinetry
work was exquisite. His restoration of old pieces
was precise and loving. Based on his ideas, he
would turn her kitchen into a functional, but
charming, workplace.

So what was eating at this gentle preacher? Ana
wondered.

"I guess you're wondering why I said that about
Stone," Rock told her as he took her hand and
guided her a few yards away from the pier and the
restaurant to a craggy rock that looked like a ready-
made bench.

"You don't have to explain," she said, taking
in their surroundings. Seagulls lifted out overhead,
searching for tidbits from the diners strolling along
the boardwalk and dunes. "I have…a very delicate
relationship with my sister, so you're allowed the
same with your brother."

"Stone…is bitter," Rock said. "He blames my
mother for our being so poor when we were growing up. You see, she gave up her inheritance to
marry our father. His name was Tillman. Everyone
called him Till. Till Dempsey, a kid from the
wrong side of Savannah. He had the audacity to
fall in love with the beautiful debutante from one
of the oldest families in Savannah." He pointed to
the big curved rock. "And he brought Eloise here
to propose to her. It's an island tradition."

A marker sign standing beside the rock stated that this was the Wedding Rock, a place where down through the centuries, sailors and fishermen had proposed to their true loves before heading out to sea. The sign also said that often couples got married here in front of the rock, their faces turned toward the ocean as they pledged their love.

"My parents were so in love, they didn't care about all that old money back in Savannah. But when my father died, my grandparents tried to make amends. They wanted us to come live with them in Savannah, but on their terms, of course. My mother refused to conform, so we stayed here in what was once the family vacation home, the house she lives in now—the only thing she accepted from her parents—and that was just so we'd have a roof over our heads. Stone got angry with her for refusing their help and their money, and I guess he never got over it. I tried to make him see that we didn't need them, but he was just twelve years old—you know, that age where peer pressure makes life so hard.

"The other kids teased us because we wore old clothes and couldn't afford the things they took for granted. Stone resented our mother for that. I rode him pretty hard back then, trying to make him see that we were going to be okay. But we weren't okay, really, and I guess I wasn't the easiest person to live with. Stone hasn't forgotten. It's not some-thing we like to talk about.''

Ana finished reading the historical marker, then turned to Rock. "If you don't like talking about this, why did you bring me here to this particular restaurant?''

"The food is good," he said with logical clarity.

"But the memories—"

"Won't go away," he finished as he tugged her down on the smooth surface of the rock. "The memories are scattered all over this island, so I quit fighting them long ago.''

Ana settled down beside him, then held her face up to catch the soft ocean breeze. The wind felt cool on her heated skin, felt good blowing over her hair. "So we both have painful memories. Why is it so hard to let go, Rock?''

"I don't know," he said, his eyes open and hon-est. "I read a quote once about old memories and young hope. I guess we cling to the sadness of the past in hopes that something better will come along and change the future.''

"You have a good memory for quotes, at least," she said, smiling. "I like that.''

"Really?" He lifted a dark brow, tilting his head toward her. "Most women find my quotes—and me—stuffy and old-fashioned.''

"I'm an old-fashioned kind of girl, remember?''

"Yes, I do recall." He leaned back against the

veined rock. "And I apologize. We didn't get to discuss business very much."

"We'll have tomorrow for business," she said. Then she ran a hand over the gray-blue rock formation. "The Wedding Rock—very romantic. I bet there are a lot of memories here."

He nodded, his eyes shimmering a deep, dark blue. "And young hope for new, better memories to come. Maybe that's why I keep coming back to this spot."

Wondering why he had taken Ana to that sad, old pier, Rock walked Ana inside her house, then checked around to make sure everything was intact.

"We rarely have any crime here on the island," he told her, hoping to reassure her. "We have a two-man police department and I think they mostly play cards and watch television all day. Or rescue a cat from a tree here and there." Then he grinned. "Besides, you strike me as a capable, independent woman."

"I already have a security system in place," she told him as she hit buttons on the code box on the hallway wall. "I learned the hard way in Savannah—my apartment got robbed once."

Rock waited, wondering what he should do or say. He was uncomfortable now that he'd revealed some of his family secrets to Ana. But she didn't seem to be holding that against him. Thinking it might be best if he just went on home, he said, "About those plans—I'll come by first thing in the morning with some sketches and ideas. I think we can have your cabinets renovated and your pantry shelves built right on time."

"Good," she said as she automatically checked the phone sitting lonely and misplaced on the hallway floor. "Oh, I have a message. Do you mind if I check it?"

"Go ahead. I need to be going, anyway."

He was about to leave, but she held up a hand while she waited for the recorder.

A feminine voice said, "Hi, Ana. It's me. Listen, I really need your help. I have to do some extensive traveling this summer—we're working on buying up a big spot of land near Atlanta for development. This just came up and I'm still trying to sell that land I own over near Savannah, so I was wondering if…well, I might need your help with the girls. I'll call you back tomorrow."

Rock watched as Ana's expression went from mild interest to a keen awareness. She seemed to stiffen, her eyes glazing over with what looked like dread. "Everything okay?" he asked, to break the silence that creaked through the old house.

Ana sighed, clicked the delete button on the message machine. "That was my sister, Tara," she said. "I have a feeling I'm about to be hit up to baby-sit all summer."

"And open a new business, too? That might be hard."

"Tara doesn't stop to think about things like that. She's a workaholic—so she expects everyone else to be the same. The only problem is, since her husband died, she's poured herself into her work even more, and now, I'm afraid she's neglecting her three daughters."

"Reminds me of my mother—and Stone, too," Rock said before thinking. "Not that he's married with children. But he works 24/7. Guess he did get a couple of my mother's traits."

"Maybe we should introduce Tara and him," Ana said with a skeptical smile. Then she added, "Don't get me wrong. Tara loves her girls. It's just been...hard on all of us since Chad died. I don't think Tara even realizes that the girls are still grieving, too. They are acting out in all sorts of ways, but she can't seem to connect on why."

"I'm sorry to hear that," Rock said, coming to lean on the wall opposite her. "But it sounds very familiar. Our mother at least understood...when our father died. She tried to comfort us, but then she got caught up in her work and we somehow learned to fend for ourselves most days. I don't know, though, if a child ever gets over that kind of grief."

Ana nodded. "That's the way it's been with the girls lately. All teenagers now, too."

"Wow. And she's going to pass them off on you?"

"I love them. And Tara doesn't trust anyone else. My parents are at that age where they travel a lot, when they aren't sick or volunteering. The girls can be a handful, so they can't keep them for more than a few days at a time. And Chad's parents live out in Texas—Ana won't let the girls go that far away over the summer. She's there with them now, for a short visit, but I doubt the girls will want to stay in Texas all summer. That leaves me, I guess."

"And me," Rock heard himself saying. "Listen, Ana, this is small island. Everyone knows everyone. We all watch out for each other. We can help with the girls."

She looked up at him, awe sparkling in her green eyes. "You'd do that...for me?"

"Of course. Mother would love it, too, I'm sure. They can swim, run around the village, learn to make pottery. There's lots to entertain teenagers here."

"You haven't met these three yet—they are eleven, thirteen and fourteen—going on thirty."

Rock leaned forward, taking in the sight of Ana standing there in the semidarkness, her fiery hair wind-tossed, the scent of the ocean still surrounding her. "If they are anything like their aunt, I can't wait to meet them."

Ana moved away, ran a hand through her hair. "Well, I have to think long and hard about this, but not tonight. It's getting late. And we have lots of work to do tomorrow."

Rock followed her to the front door. "Back to business, right?"

"Yes, business is what brought me here. But I did enjoy dinner."

"Even though I told you all about the Dempsey family dysfunctions?"

"Every family has dysfunctions, as you can see from my sister's phone call."

"Maybe so. But, Ana, I want you to understand. I love my mother and my brothers—they mean the world to me. And since becoming a minister, I've learned we can't control other people. We can only control how we react to them, and we have to leave the rest in God's hands."

She glanced down at the phone. "It's hard to do that."

"Yes, it is. But we can do the next-best thing. We love them—unconditionally, sometimes with trepidation, sometimes with a bit of anger and resentment, but always, knowing that if family needs us, we have to come through."

"Like me, with my sister? I should tell her yes, bring the girls to me?"

"If that's what you want to do in your heart."

"I love those three. I've always wanted children."

"You might be the best thing for them right now. A good, positive role model."

"Me?" She scoffed, shook her head. "I'm just their old-maid aunt who loves art and reading and cooking. I'm the plain sister, Rock, in case you haven't figured that out yet."

He leaned close again, one hand on the old brass doorknob. "Oh, I've figured out a lot of things about you, Ana. And I'm looking forward to working through the rest."

He heard her sigh.

"The rest?"

"The rest of what makes Ana Hanson such an interesting, pretty woman."

"Interesting and pretty describes my outgoing, dynamic sister, not me."

"I don't recall asking you about your sister. I'm only interested in getting to know you. And you are by no means plain."

"Really, Rock, there's not much to me."

Rock reached up, pushed at a burnished curl clinging to her cheek. "There's more than you know, Ana. Much more."

Ana stepped back, away from his touch. "Remember, you were hired to work on restoring my cabinets, not me."

Rock could tell she was scared, uncomfortable. He felt much the same way. And he still wasn't sure where all of this might lead. "Fair enough," he said. "But I've learned something about restoration over the years. Sometimes, if we keep polishing and pampering, we find true treasures underneath all the dirt and dust and neglect."

"You're talking in riddles again."

"I'm telling it like it is," he replied as he backed out the door. "You are a treasure, Ana. And somebody needs to show you that."

She just smiled and said, "Thank you. You're awfully sweet to try and make me feel better."

Then she closed the door. Rock could hear the *click* of the lock, effectively shutting him out of her life for now.

"You should feel better," he thought. "Someone needs to show you how special you are." Rock decided that he was just the man for the job.

Chapter Four

"I invited Ana to dinner tonight—with you and me."

Rock stared across the workshop at his mother. "That explains this surprise visit."

Eloise rarely came to his workshop. She rarely left the compound of her home and studio. And she never cooked. Her groceries, housekeeping and other essentials, including real cooked meals, were now taken care of by a capable couple that lived in a small cottage near her property.

Rock had been pleased, but curious, when his mother had waltzed into the workshop this morning. Now he understood, of course. Eloise was up to matchmaking again.

"What if I have plans?"

"You never have plans, Rock. When was the last time you actually dated anyone?"

He had to stop and think. "I paid a visit to a single woman just the other night."

Eloise lifted a finger, wagging it at him. "You've been watching wrestling on Saturday nights with old Miss McPherson again, haven't you, son? That doesn't count."

"Okay, it's been a while. But you know how it is, Mom. I work."

Eloise picked up a plywood pattern. "Getting in your digs early today?"

"I'm sorry. Like mother, like son, I reckon. I guess I have been working too hard lately. What time is dinner? And what is Neda cooking?"

Eloise smiled at that. "Around seven, and we're having a picnic out on the grounds—barbecued chicken, potato salad, the works. Ana told me once she loved picnics."

"I'll keep that in mind," Rock replied while he set his router flush with the base of a piece of wood, then lined up for the cut. Dropping his protective goggles on, he proceeded to cut the fresh-smelling walnut wood.

Eloise waited patiently, her hands folded over the front of her long linen skirt. When Rock had finished, she said, "Is that for Ana's kitchen?"

"Yep. I'm having to replace some of the original wood—the back sections of some of the cabinets just aren't sturdy anymore. Not to mention that most of the upper units need reinforcement." He lifted his head toward the sections of what would soon be an island station in the kitchen. "Don Ashworth and his son, Cal, have been helping me with that monster. But they took the morning off—Cal's getting his driver's license."

Eloise said, "Oh, I saw Greta Epperson at the town hall meeting about the lighthouse fund-raiser. She said rumor has it you and Ana were having dinner at the Sunken Pier a couple of nights ago."

Rock lifted his gaze to the heavens. "Oh, great. I guess that news flash will grace the gossip page in this week's paper. And it probably won't matter that it was a *business* dinner."

Eloise chuckled, then eyed the pieces that had yet to be put together inside Ana's house. "Not to Greta. She loves trailing a good story and embellishing on the facts. And speaking of business, you're doing a good job, according to Ana."

"She hasn't complained so far. Besides, she's been busy training her staff and testing recipes. She's got to get her menu down just right—she's a stickler for details."

"I want to hear the details of how things are progressing between you two, and I don't mean the working relationship. I'd rather hear it from you than that pesky Greta."

Staying tight-lipped, Rock picked up a hand

plane and started passing it over a piece of wood he'd shaped into a crown molding. He wasn't about to go into detail about Ana with his overly inquisitive mother.

Yet Eloise asked, anyway. "Do you like her?"

Pretending to misunderstand, Rock nodded toward the new cabinets. "This one—she's coming along nicely."

Eloise scoffed, kicked at sawdust. "You know perfectly well I'm not talking about cabinets. How are things with Ana?"

Rock stopped the pressure he'd been applying to the hand plane. "Things with Ana are...business as usual."

He wouldn't tell Eloise that the week he'd spent working for Ana had left him disturbed and excited. He liked knowing Ana was in the next room, working, sometimes humming, at her desk. He liked hearing her laughing and talking with her two capable sidekicks, Jackie and Tina. He enjoyed hearing the women talk about their families and their stressful days. He even enjoyed trying to figure out the secret codes women use to convey message. He suspected, from some of the sly, smiling looks the women gave him in passing, that some of those codes were used to throw him off. Or maybe drive him crazy.

But Rock didn't ask for explanations. He worked silently, or with Don and Cal by his side.

He worked steadily, since they only had a few weeks left before the opening. He couldn't tell his mother that he went to bed each night with the scent of Ana's floral perfume wafting through his senses. He couldn't explain that when he went down to the beach for a midnight run, his thoughts always turned to the time he'd spent in Ana's kitchen, measuring and hammering, tearing out and replacing.

And the whole time, he'd felt as if he'd been tearing away at his own old hurts and replacing them with something good and pure. Only, other than cooking him wonderful, dainty lunches so she could test her menu, Ana was keeping her distance. And keeping busy.

Which meant he couldn't wait to see her tonight at dinner. But he didn't dare tell his mother that.

Eloise was watching him in that calm, disconcerting way she had. It was the same way in which she'd stare at a piece of ancient wood or jagged stone and see things no one else could even begin to imagine. Rock wondered what she saw when she looked at him.

"Mother, I'll be there. So you can quit glaring at me."

"I love your face," his mother said. "You have a noble face, Rock."

"Thank you."

"You don't want to talk to me, do you."

"I'm busy, is all. Got to finish these pieces and get started on a few others. Time marches on."

"You don't like me interfering."

"Never have."

"I've tried to stay out of your love life, but there's something about Ana."

Rock wiped the sweat off his brow, then looked at his mother. "On that, at least, we can agree."

"Then, you do…like her?"

"We're not going steady yet, but yes, I like her."

"So a mother can hope."

The old anger surfaced as quickly and swiftly as a rebel wave hitting the shore. "Why does this matter so much to you, anyway?"

Eloise's stark eyes opened wide. Rock saw the mist of tears there. "I know I failed you, Rock. I was…alone, afraid, obsessed with making a name for myself. I…believe God has given me another chance. I intend to see that chance through."

"By pushing your oldest, bachelor son off on the first woman who shows him the slightest hint of attention?"

"You've dated other women, so don't put yourself down." She shook her head. "I'm just hoping and praying that you and Ana make a good match. I want you to be happy, truly happy, and Ana seems perfect for you. Everyone should have the chance to know pure happiness in their life."

Rock saw the light leave his mother's beautiful eyes, and he knew she was remembering. He hated himself for being harsh with her. He couldn't touch her. He couldn't bring himself to hug her. But he did give her his full attention. "I'd like that, Mother. I'd like to have that just once in my life."

Eloise's expression changed to a smile. "I'll see you at seven, then."

Ana stepped out of her car, a warm apple pie in one hand and her crocheted purse in the other. Closing the car door with a sandaled foot, she stared up at the imposing Victorian beach house that sat nestled underneath billowing live oaks across from the sandy curve of the shore.

The house was an aged white, battered from years of tropical winds and salty mists. Its shutters were a muted gray, its many lace-curtained windows thrown open to the sea. Around back, past the sandy, shell-covered drive, stood Eloise's studio.

She heard laughter coming from the garden, so Ana headed through the carriage drive on the side of the house to find Eloise and Rock talking with another, older couple.

Eloise turned as she heard the crunch of Ana's footsteps. "Ana! You made it."

"And brought pie," Rock said, his smile gentle, his eyes keen on her.

Ana managed a shaky smile, and wondered why she'd gone to such great pains with her appearance. Upswept hair, a sundress with brilliant tropical flowers splashed across its gathered skirts, a dash of lipstick and perfume. From the look in Rock's eyes, she'd done a passable job, at least. That pleased and aggravated her at the same time.

But then, this past week had been full of such moments—sweet and torturing all at the same time. She had found herself, on more than one occasion, stopping to watch Rock while he worked. He'd looked like every woman's dream in his faded T-shirt and even more faded jeans, his heavy work boots clunking on her polished floors, his dark, curling hair sprinkled with sawdust.

"Why do carpenters always look so yummy?" Jackie had asked just yesterday, grinning.

"And they are so good with their hands," Tina, petite and buxom, had said through a sigh.

"Why don't you two get back to work?" Ana had retorted, her own smile belying the stern tone in her voice. She had to agree with her new helpers. Rock looked good working, and he felt good each time his fingers brushed over hers in passing or his arm touched hers as they met in the doorway.

But what Ana had enjoyed the most didn't really have anything to do with Rock's physical appearance. It was his eyes, his facial expressions, that

tugged at her heart and made her want to get to
know him better. He'd go from intense concentra-
tion to thoughtful contemplation, his blue eyes
changing color like a sea in the sun with each new
calculation, with each touch of hammer to nail.
Rock truly loved his work. And it showed in the
beautiful cabinets he was recreating in her kitchen.

"Want me to take that?" he asked now, bringing Ana out of her thoughts.

She glanced down at the pie she still held in one
hand. "Oh, yes. Thanks."

"Smells wonderful," he said under his breath,
his eyes on her instead of the pie.

Ana allowed a little shiver of pure delight to
move like falling mist down her spine. Rock flirted
in such a subtle, quiet way, it sometimes took her
a few minutes to even realize he *was* doing it. But
he was doing it—flirting with her. And tonight, she
intended to enjoy it.

"We're eating in the garden," Eloise told her
as she guided Ana to a lacy black wrought-iron
table and matching chairs centered near a cluster
of vivid red-tipped firebush.

As Ana glanced around, a hummingbird buzzed
near the tall, bright shrubs. "It's such a lovely
night."

"Yes, it is," Rock said, his gaze once again
moving over Ana's face and hair. "You look
great."

"Thanks." She hated the way she automatically patted at her hair.

He just stood there, his hands in the pockets of his khaki walking shorts. The man sure cleaned up nicely. The light blue polo shirt only made his eyes seem darker. And he didn't smell half-bad himself—like the sea on a fresh crisp morning.

Ana swallowed, dropped her purse on the nearest chair. "What can I do to help with dinner?"

Eloise motioned to the man and woman hovering over the smoking grill. "Not a thing. Neda and Cy Wilson, meet Ana Hanson. Ana, these two are the cooks around here."

"Among other things," Rock said with a wry smile.

Ana waved to the couple. "Hello."

They both shouted a greeting.

"Hope you're hungry," Cy said, his jovial grin full of leathery wrinkles. "Neda cooked enough for a small army."

"I'll do my best to eat my fair share," Ana replied.

Neda, a short, gray-haired woman, nodded. "You look like you could use a good meal."

Rock laughed, his glance moving over Ana. "Ana happens to be a very good cook herself."

Neda came over to stand by them. "I hear you're opening a tea room. That sounds lovely."

Ana immediately felt at home with the tiny

woman. "I hope it will be a hit. The island seemed like the perfect spot, based on our research."

"We get a lot of tourists, of course," Cy said as he lifted the grill lid to check on the sizzling chicken. "The ladies should like that. Shopping and lunch—ain't that what women like most?"

Eloise waved a hand. "Not all the time. Believe it or not, some women actually prefer work to shopping and eating."

"I sure hope not all of them. I need customers," Ana replied, acutely aware of Rock's gaze as he looked with a frown from his mother to her. She always got a strange, unsettling impression whenever she talked about her ambitions with him. He seemed interested, yet she sensed a hesitation in him, as if he wasn't quite listening. Did Rock disapprove of a woman in business?

It didn't matter if he approved or not. She was in this for the duration and she had to make it work—she had to make a living somehow. She'd wagered everything on this venture, including giving in to her sister's insistence that Ana let her help finance the whole thing. Ana wouldn't be able to hold her head up if she failed Tara. In spite of their often strained relationship, she loved her sister.

That made her think about the girls.

Rock touched her arm. "Have you decided?"

"About what?"

"About your nieces coming for the summer."

"Can you read my mind?"

He gave her a long, measuring look, as if he truly were trying to do just that. "No. It's just that we talked about this earlier, after you got another phone call, remember? You were worried then, and you have that same look on your face now."

"I do remember," she replied, thinking back to her long conversation with Tara earlier today. "And yes, I guess I've decided. My sister came through for me with the financing of the tea room. I intend to come through for her and the girls. Tara needs my help now more than ever."

"You're a good sister."

"No, not really. Just trying to make amends."

"Now, what could you possibly have to make amends for?"

"You'd be surprised."

He grinned, offered her a tall glass of tea with lemon. "You do have that tendency to…surprise me, that is. Take tonight, for example. I was sure you wouldn't show up."

"And why wouldn't I?" She took a drink of the syrupy sweet tea, glad for the liquid on her suddenly dry throat.

"Business, remember?" He winked, lowered his voice. "In case you haven't noticed, my dear mother is trying very hard to throw us together. I've tried to explain we have a good, solid *working* relationship. Wouldn't want to ruin that."

His eyes indicated that he'd love to ruin that.

Ana set her glass down. She didn't miss the bit of sarcasm in his words. "So because of that, you thought I'd refuse to come to dinner? You thought maybe I'd just work straight through the weekend?"

"Yep. You've made it pretty clear—"

"A girl has to eat."

"And a girl shouldn't be all alone on a warm Friday night."

"True." She pushed at her hair, tried to hide her disappointment that he considered their relationship just *working,* that perhaps he considered her a workaholic—then reminded herself that she wanted it that way, too. "As long as we have an understanding," she said, just to back up her feelings.

"We do. Monday through Friday, we work." He leaned close, so close she could smell the scent of sandalwood and spice around him. "But come Friday night, I might be inclined to ask you to take a long stroll along the beach with me after dinner."

His words implied they'd be doing this more often—having dinner together on a Friday night. That left Ana feeling light-headed and more confused than ever. So she tried to counter. "To talk business, right?"

"No, ma'am. Just to talk—about you, about me,

about anything but cabinets and remodeling kitchens and opening tea rooms.''

''What if we find we have nothing else to talk about?''

''Then, we can do something besides talking, I reckon.''

She swallowed again, felt the heat rising up her back in spite of the balmy breeze. ''That could… be a serious mistake.''

''Could be. Might be pleasant, though.''

Ana watched his face—that expressive face that lingered in her mind long after the lights were out. He seemed determined to make her blush, to make her feel things she didn't need to be feeling. Yet he seemed almost to be testing her. Did he find her a challenge? Did he think he could turn her head, make her forget about work and obligations, maybe just to prove a point?

He's a distraction, Ana. A big one. A big, handsome, kind, considerate, intriguing, puzzling, distraction. You don't need that kind of distraction right now. You need to focus on the tea room.

And the girls. They'd be coming next week.

Suddenly, Ana smiled. With three rambunctious, inquisitive teenagers in the house, she wouldn't have time to dream about Rock Dempsey. Even on a lonely Friday night.

''After dinner,'' he whispered, making her forget everything she'd just thought, as the feather of his words moved over her ear and hair with a heart-stopping warmth.

"What?" she managed to whisper back.

"We're going for that walk on the beach."

"Are you sure that's wise? I mean, won't your mother get the wrong idea?"

"No, I think she'll get the right idea. I have to hand it to her, she's right on target with this one."

"What do you mean?"

"I mean," he said as he reached out a hand to tug her toward the wonderful-smelling food, "she said she hoped we'd make a good match. I'm inclined to agree with her on that. At least, I'm hoping, too."

Ana knew she was crossing a line here. If she let this go any farther, it would be so hard to turn back.

"And…what about our *working* relationship? What if things get messy?"

Rock nudged her toward the table. "Well, there's work and there's play. I try never to confuse the two."

Before Ana could respond, Eloise announced dinner and asked Rock to say grace. A few minutes later, Ana listened to his deep, baritone voice as he thanked God for all their many blessings, and wondered if he'd still feel the same toward her when her work started getting in the way of their play. Would she fail the Rock Dempsey test of the perfect woman?

It didn't matter if he was testing her. It didn't matter that she found him attractive. She had to put her business, and now the girls, first.

And Rock Dempsey would just have to see that, whether he approved or not.

Chapter Five

❧

Rock stood on the steps of the Sunset Chapel, taking in the stormy morning. "Probably won't get many takers today, Lord," he said out loud. It looked like a long, rainy Sunday.

"A good day for a nap," Reverend Pal would have said.

Rock thought about the long day ahead and wondered how Ana would spend it. Now, why did he have to think of her? Why, indeed? Maybe because they *had* gone for that walk on the beach after dinner the other night? Maybe because he'd enjoyed being with her, making her laugh, watching the way the moonlight washed her copper-colored hair in shimmering hues of gold. And maybe because he had issued her a challenge of sorts, a challenge about which he was now having serious doubts.

Rock remembered the feel of her hand in his, the way her expressive green eyes lit up when she smiled. Then he remembered her dogged determination to make her tea room a success. Nothing wrong there, except that he'd vowed not to get involved with a woman too much like his mother.

But was Ana like his mother? Certainly not in looks. Ana was pretty, not in the exotic way Eloise was beautiful, but pretty in a girl-next-door kind of way that Rock liked. Ana could cook, too. That gave her points in Rock's book. But her cooking revolved around her career. He couldn't forget that.

Rock shook his head, glanced up as church members started appearing, some walking underneath umbrellas, others driving to avoid the coming storm.

Greta Epperson greeted him from underneath a bright pansy-bordered umbrella. "Morning, Preacher Rock. How's the cabinet business?"

Her sly grin told him she was fishing for more than an update on his work habits. With her big round black-framed glasses and stark white bobbed hair, she reminded him of an owl.

"Business is good," he told her, smiling. "But then, you probably already know exactly how good, right, Greta?"

"I hear things. Very interesting things." Greta grinned, shook his hand, then went on inside.

His mother walked up, smiled, patted his cheek, then found a seat near Greta. They whispered and chuckled, their heads close together.

His mother was too smug. It irritated him that he was actually doing something Eloise approved of. Thinking that was no way for a preacher to act, Rock sent up a prayer for patience and forgiveness. He needed to cut his mother some slack. After all, she had three grown sons and wanted them all married with families.

Rock hadn't thought too much about a family. He'd pretty much given up after a few false starts with women who wanted to move to the city. Rock would never leave Sunset Island. He was too set in his ways, and too attached to this place. It would take a special woman to understand and accept that about him.

He thought of Ana. She'd left the city to come to the island. That earned her points, too. Smiling and shaking the hands of more of his congregation, Rock decided he'd better concentrate on his sermon for this morning and quit worrying about his feelings for Ana Hanson. Because right now, it was obvious Ana needed to stay centered on her business. And that made it even more obvious that Rock needed to remember his pledge to never get involved with a career woman. Or a woman in the arts, for that matter.

That was two strikes against Ana.

But when Rock looked up to find her car coming up the winding drive, he felt his heart crash against his rib cage with the ferocity of the distant thunder clashing in the sky. When she got out, all fresh-faced and dressed in a dainty white dress sprinkled with green and blue flowers, Rock couldn't seem to remember exactly why he should steer clear of her.

So he stood there, debating with his soul.

Career woman, art patron, work-focused.

Pretty woman, good cook, great smelling, great smile.

A nice lady.

A nice, available single woman.

A woman who was now smiling at him as she ignored the mist of rain falling around her. *This* version won out. How could he turn away from a woman who didn't seem to mind her hair getting wet?

"Ana," he said in a rush of breath. "Welcome."

"I hope you don't mind," she said as she came up the steps. "I was just feeling so lonely…and even though I have a ton of work to do—"

"It's the Sabbath," Rock said. "You're allowed

a day of rest. And I never mind it when I get a prospective new church member."

She stopped on the steps, just underneath the overhang. Rock resisted the urge to reach up and wipe a drop of rain off her curling hair. "I've always attended church on and off," she said, smiling. "I guess I could use some encouragement in that department though."

Waving to other people, Rock guided her through the planked double doors inside the tiny chapel. "Savannah has a lot of gracious, old churches."

Ana nodded, glanced around at the simple furnishings. "This one is as beautiful as any I've seen there," she said, her words hushed, her eyes wide.

"It's been here for centuries," Rock explained. "The pews are made of cypress, as are the beams in the ceiling. If you look very closely up near the altar, you'll find bullet holes from both the Revolutionary War and the Civil War. Even though Savannah fell during the Revolutionary War, toward the end the 'Swamp Fox' outfoxed the British up and down the South Carolina coast and all around these parts. Then, almost a century later, Sherman marched to the sea, and after giving Savannah to Abraham Lincoln as a Christmas present, he allowed some of his soldiers to pass by here on their way back up north. But we're still standing."

"Amazing," Ana said, clearly impressed. "I love the history of this island."

"There's lots more," Rock said, pleased that she was indeed an old-fashioned kind of girl. That got her more points, too. Not that he was keeping a tally. Anyway, he thought to himself, the pros were fast outweighing the cons in this relationship.

Feeling a bit better now, he thought he might be able to handle this, if he kept his head. It wouldn't hurt to keep Ana company, to enjoy picnics and sitting on the beach with her. Wouldn't hurt at all.

"Why are you grinning at me?" Ana asked, causing Rock to snap to attention.

"Was I? I guess I'm just glad you came."

"Your mother suggested I might enjoy one of your sermons."

"Oh, so you only came to please my mother?"

"No. I came because I wanted to. To hear you preach."

"I don't preach, really. Mostly just spout philosophy and couple that with Bible lessons. I'll probably make you to fall asleep."

"I doubt that."

The look she gave him made Rock swallow and stall out. What if Ana took things way more seriously between them than he was planning? What would he do then?

Rock couldn't answer that question. He had to give his sermon. Beside he doubted Ana would have much time for him, what with three girls coming for the summer and Ana opening a new business.

In fact, this relationship should work out perfectly. Ana was too busy for a love life, and Rock, well, he was too wary to let down his guard. They could coast along, as friends and companions, for a very long time. He'd enjoy home-cooked meals, her pretty smile, and knowing he had a friend who would please Eloise enough to keep her off his back. Ana would get companionship, a mentor and a friend, and a man who was determined to respect the boundaries they obviously needed between them. A perfect arrangement.

Almost too perfect, Rock concluded just before he stepped up into the pulpit.

He had looked perfect and sounded even better, Ana thought after Rock had finished his sermon. Was it right and fair that a man of God could dress in a striped polo shirt and casual slacks and still look so fine? Was it good and great that what he said about the wisdom of Psalm 42—the one about hope in God's love—made sense and kept her interest even while she kept wondering what it would be like to kiss him? Did it matter that she'd seen him every day for the past week, but she had to have one more hour with him on Sunday?

Lord forgive me, but that's why I came here.

Ana wasn't proud of that confession, but it was the truth. She'd woken up this morning, restless and blue. Not even working on inventory or polishing already shining furniture had given her any peace.

She'd wanted to see Rock again. And she'd been pleasantly surprised that he had seemed pleased to see *her* again. Ana knew this was tentative. She knew that Rock had reservations about a relationship with her. Well, she felt the same—interested but cautious. Maybe that was the best way to go into this.

Thinking back over the years since she'd been dumped in college, Ana could see that her dealings with the opposite sex had been pitiful and sad, to say the least. She'd always tried to rush things. That hadn't worked, so she'd given up. Now she was a bit rusty in the dating department. All the more reason to be cautious, but hopeful, just as Rock's sermon had suggested.

"I hope you come back."

The lilting voice beside Ana pulled her back to reality. She turned to find a tiny woman in a big straw hat with a giant sunflower on it staring up at her through eyes surrounded by wrinkles.

"I just might," Ana said, smiling. She took the aged hand the woman extended. "I'm Ana, Ana Hanson."

"The tea room lady," the woman replied, her

thin lips pursing as she scrutinized Ana. "The one the preacher there's been seen around the island with."

"Uh, yes, I guess that's me, but—"

"I'm Mildred McPherson. Known Roderick Dempsey since he was knee-high to a June bug. He's a good boy."

Ana had to smile at Rock being called a "boy." "He seems like a good person."

"He watches basketball and wrestling with me on Saturday nights."

"Oh, really?" Sensing a tad of womanly jealousy here, Ana could only nod. "I…didn't realize he's a wrestling fan."

"He mostly just sits there and watches me," the little old lady said, preening as she touched her hat. "I get a bit carried away."

"I see."

"He's probably afraid I'll have a stroke or something."

"Wouldn't want that."

"Honey, I'll be eighty-one next month. A stroke is the least of my worries. I can assure you, I am fully prepared to meet my Maker."

Completely nonplussed by this tiny dynamo, Ana glanced around, glad to find Rock walking down the aisle toward them.

"I see you've met Milly," he said to Ana.

"Yes. We were just talking about…wrestling."

Rock grinned. "Ah, yes. Milly's one vice."

"I just watch, is all," Milly said, her expression stubborn. "Besides, at my age, there aren't many vices left."

Rock patted the little woman on the back. "Ana, Milly McPherson is one of the finest Christian women you will ever meet. And she can cook like a dream." He motioned to Ana. "Ana can cook, too. You two should compare recipes."

"I'd love that," Ana said, relaxing now that Rock had joined the conversation. "I could put some of your recipes on the menu at the tea room. You'd get full credit, of course."

"I'd expect full credit," Milly retorted. "We might can talk. People do say my Brunswick stew is the best this side of Atlanta."

"Oh, that would make a great dish for winter."

"Or a rainy day like this one," Milly countered. Then she leaned close. "I just happen to have a slow-cooker full back home. You're welcome to come to Sunday dinner and try it for yourself." Then she stretched her head toward Rock. "You too, of course, Preacher."

Ana felt a sudden panic. Another meal with Rock. But then, she would like to test that stew. "That's very kind of you."

"Take it or leave it," Milly replied tartly as she started up the aisle toward the door. "Twelve-thirty sharp—that's when I eat. I have to have my beauty nap, you know.''

"We'll be there," Rock called. Then he turned to Ana, a grin splitting his face. "Don't you just love her?"

"Uh…yes, sure," Ana said, smiling. "But is it just me, or does she intimidate everyone?"

"She does, indeed. Crusty and full of a viper's wit, but good as gold. Mildred McPherson was a schoolteacher—retired now, of course. But she has struck fear in the hearts of many an island child, including my brothers and me."

"But you seem close to her now." At his perplexed expression, she added, "Wrestling?"

"Oh, that. I just enjoy watching Milly enjoying herself. I get a kick out of her competitive spirit."

"She made it quite clear your Saturday nights are usually occupied—watching her watch wrestling."

"I just go by to check on her from time to time," he said as they strolled down the aisle. The chapel was empty now. Leading her out onto the porch, Rock turned to lock the door. "Miss McPherson lives down the street from me. She cooks for me, mentors me, fusses at me, and keeps me on the straight and narrow."

"Miss? She's a spinster?"

"Some would say. I prefer calling her a lovely *mature* maiden."

"Oh, I meant no disrespect. But I can certainly understand why she might not have married."

"Think she scared all of her suitors away?"

"Most definitely."

The rain had stopped, leaving a cool mist in the afternoon air. Ana waited for Rock to finish locking up, then said, "Do you think going to her house for lunch is wise?"

"It's a necessary function of life. George Bernard Shaw said there is no love sincerer than the love of food."

Ana saw the stubborn glint in his eyes and once again got the distinct feeling that he somehow disapproved of her, even when he was flirting.

"My point exactly," she said. "You seem to migrate toward women who can feed you. Should I be worried about that?"

Rock glanced across the narrow ribbon of road between the church and the shore. "Think I'm using you for cooking purposes?"

She thought back on the past week. He'd personally tested every one of her menu recipes, and he'd asked for seconds several times. "Are you?"

He shook his head. "I can't lie. I like a woman who can cook."

Ana put her hands on her hips, a narrow thread of defiance coursing up her spine. Was this it, then? It would certainly explain why she'd felt as if she were being tested.

"Is that a prerequisite?"

"To what?"

"To…dating? Have you been testing me, Rock, to see if I fit your idea of what a woman should be?"

"What if it is? What if I have? Would that be a problem for you?"

"I don't know. You said there's work and there's play, and you never confuse the two. But I think you are confused about me. My cooking is my work. And I don't like being used…while you play."

"I didn't say that. You have misunderstood the situation. And besides, *you* offered me samples of everything you cooked. Are you mad about that now?"

Whirling in a stance of feminine fire, she said, "No, not at all, since we obviously aren't *dating*. I'm just glad I found this out now."

He was right behind her. "Good, I'm glad, too. A man has a right to demand some things in life."

She pivoted and butted right into his chest. "*Demand?* Did you say *demand?*"

"I believe so, yes."

"So you're telling me that you will demand a woman knows how to cook before you'll even consider—"

He gave a gentle tug, pulling her so close that she could see the flecks of black in his blue eyes.

"Before I'd consider dating her…kissing her, maybe?"

His gaze moved from her eyes to her mouth.

Ana's breath lodged inside her throat. "What if I told you I wouldn't dream of dating, much less *kissing,* a man who'd make such a demand?"

His eyes still on her lips, he said, "I guess that wouldn't matter, since we're not dating. And since I'm not about to kiss you."

Disappointment overtook fury in Ana's heart. "Oh, well then—"

Before she could finish, he did kiss her. His mouth came down on hers like rain hitting sand, fast and swift. At first Ana tried to pull away, but his hands on her back held her still. And the feel of his lips on hers held her suspended between want and need, between rage and calm. She returned the kiss with one of her own.

Just to show him she could do more than cook.

Until Rock lifted his head and stared down at her as if she'd bitten him.

"What—" Ana asked, breathless.

"I am so sorry," he said, backing away. "I don't know what came over me."

Ana stepped back too, fists at her side. "It's all right. It…I…we…I'd better just go on home."

"What about Miss McPherson's stew?"

Just like a man to think of food—especially *this* man.

She turned, her head down in mortification. She'd certainly lost her appetite. "I'll taste the stew another time." He regretted kissing her. Rock regretted his actions. Well, shouldn't she regret it, too?

No, I can't regret something that felt so good, so right, she thought bitterly. But she knew it could never happen again. Rock obviously had some issues to work through and she didn't have time to help him.

"Ana?"

She heard Rock calling her, but Ana kept walking to her car, wet sand kicking up with each step to smear on her bare legs.

"Ana, come back, please?"

Ana couldn't look at him.

She opened the car door, only to have it slammed shut by a big, strong hand.

"Ana," he said, her name like a plea on the wind. "Ana, I'm sorry."

"Would you just stop apologizing," she said. "Look, it's bad enough that we got in a fight over who does the cooking. And it's even worse that you were forced to kiss me to prove a point."

"I wasn't trying to prove anything," Rock said, his hand on her arm, his eyes holding hers. "Look, I'm a big dolt, okay? I'm too old-fashioned for my own good."

"Because you *demand* that a woman should cook for you?"

He winced. "You make me sound like a male chauvinist monster."

"Not a monster, Rock. And I know you're not a male chauvinist. Just a man who knows what he wants in a relationship. No shame in that."

But she could see the shame in his eyes. He looked so sheepish, Ana instantly wished she could just fall through the earth. "Honestly, it's good to know where we stand. At least now I know what to expect. Not that I expected anything."

Could this get any worse?

It did.

Rain started coming down in mean, stinging drops. Huge, mad drops. Before she even thought of getting the car door open, Ana was soaked.

"Now look what you've done!" she shouted to Rock.

"Me?" He held his hands in the air. "Believe it or not, Ana, although I might make certain demands, I can't bring about rain with the snap of my fingers."

"Well, you have connections up there, don't you?" she asked, pointing a dripping wet finger toward the dark heavens.

"Not that kind," Rock countered. Then he reached for her hand. "Let's get inside, out of this storm, okay?"

"Good idea." She turned for her car. "I'm going home—to fix my own lunch."

Rock tugged her around. "No, come on inside, to my house."

"I will not."

"You're getting soaked."

"I don't care. I can dry off at home."

"Ana, please. So I can explain."

"There is nothing to explain. You've made yourself perfectly clear. Since I've met you, I've felt you've been judging me, testing me in some way. Now I know you were only trying to find out what I had in my pantry."

He looked dazed for a minute. "But you *like* to cook."

"Yes, I do," she said over the sound of pelting rain. "But that doesn't mean I want a man telling me I *have* to do it."

"*Women,*" Rock said, dragging her by the hand toward his cottage. "You have to listen to reason."

"Let me go!"

"I will not let you go home mad and wet."

Stomping up onto his porch, Ana pushed drenched hair off her face. "You probably just want me to come inside to fix your Sunday dinner!"

Groaning in frustration, Rock yanked her into his arms, bringing her clinging-clothed body close to his. "I only want you here for one reason, Ana."

And then he showed her that reason.

He kissed her again, wet lips to wet lips.

Ana sighed and fell against him, a soft, radiating warmth spreading through her heart.

Well, at least he wasn't thinking about food *right now*.

Chapter Six

Food was the farthest thing from Rock's mind. But he was preparing lunch for Ana, anyway. And wondering the whole time why he'd gone and done a foolish thing like kiss the woman.

Maybe because she made him mad and glad at the same time. Maybe because he'd wanted to kiss her, even when he was trying to reason with her. And he *would* make her listen to reason, Rock thought as he slapped together bread and chicken salad.

That is, if she ever came out of the bathroom.

After their second kiss out on the porch, he'd finally convinced her to come inside, out of the cold and wet. She'd been shivering—maybe from the rain, maybe because their kiss seemed to affect her just as much as it had him—Rock couldn't be sure. And he wasn't too sure about where they might go from here. But he did know he'd made a big mess of things and he still had work to do at Ana's place. He wanted to smooth things out, so they wouldn't have any more scenes such as this.

If she ever spoke to him again.

A few minutes later, the door down the hall opened and Ana emerged, dressed in his heavy bathrobe, her damp hair combed and her face fresh-scrubbed. "Thanks…for the robe," she said timidly, her eyes downcast.

"You're welcome," he said, his eyes on her in his robe. Maybe he should have had her put on a shirt and some sweat pants instead. The faded blue robe swallowed her and made her look sweet and vulnerable. And *kissable.*

And he couldn't kiss her again.

Help me, Lord, Rock silently prayed, appealing to heaven for strength. He'd made two big mistakes today. One, implying he needed a woman who could cook for him, and two, kissing the very woman who could cook for him, but didn't want to.

And forcing her to come inside his cottage to get into dry clothes had been an even worse decision.

"Go on into the den," he said, his back turned.

"I built a fire. This rain has brought a chill to the air."

"Thank you."

He didn't dare turn around. Instead he waited, holding his breath and wondering if he'd done the right thing by bringing Ana here. Then he heard her sharp intake of breath.

Rock couldn't take it anymore. Picking up the tray of sandwiches and fruit, he hurried into the wide, multi-windowed den that allowed a sweeping view of the distant ocean.

And found Ana clutching her hands to his robe as if the material were a lifeboat. She turned at the sound of his footfalls. Turned and sent him a look somewhere between amazement and frustration. "What have you done?"

Rock shrugged, wishing he knew how to handle her. "My mother told me you like picnics. So I—"

"Made a picnic," she said, finishing his sentence. "Right here on the floor in front of the fire."

"Yeah." He looked down at the checkered blanket and tattered tapestry throw pillows he'd tossed down on the wooden floor. He'd grabbed the flowers from the porch—thank goodness Miss McPherson insisted on bringing him geraniums—and he'd strewn the mismatched plates, silverware and chipped glasses in what he hoped was a passable setting. He'd finished it off with a battered, sputtering candle he'd used a few weeks ago when the electricity had gone out, as it often did during rainstorms.

"Why did you do this?"

Her question was accusing, suspicious.

Rock felt as he'd been pinned to the wall. "I…I felt bad about our…misunderstanding. I wanted to make it up to you."

She glanced at the tray of food in his hands. "What's that?"

"Chicken-salad sandwiches. Some grapefruit and orange sections. A couple of strawberries, and some cheese." He shrugged. "It's not much, but the chicken salad is fresh."

Ana eyed his concoction with a look of disdain. "Did you make it yourself?"

Rock brought the tray to the wooden coffee table. "As a matter of fact, I did. Canned chicken, walnuts and celery. A little mayonnaise and a touch of mustard."

Ana sniffed the air, her chin lifted. "Sounds okay."

"Then, have a seat on the blanket," Rock replied, knowing he sounded as curt and distant as she seemed.

The phone rang, and, glad for the distraction, Rock grabbed it from its cradle on the hallway table. "Hello?"

It was Miss McPherson. "You're late."

Rock glanced at Ana. "Uh, we had a bit of a

problem. We got soaked in the rainstorm. Decided to just have a sandwich here instead. Sorry I didn't call. I got busy—''

"You like her, don't you."

He took a breath, willed himself to say the right thing. "I'm not sure about that, but we'll see."

"Yep, you got it bad. Must have put you in a regular tizzy. You never pass up my Brunswick stew."

Rock winced, wondering if Ana was right about him, after all. Maybe he did only hang around women who could feed him, regardless of their age or status. But, stubbornly, he refused to change now.

"Save me a bowlful?"

"I'll put you a pint or two in the freezer. Good-bye."

The dial tone tolled like a ship horn in Rock's head. Replaying the phone in its cradle, he turned back to Ana. "Milly is going to save us some stew."

"That's nice."

He hated the civility of this conversation, hated the stilted way Ana was holding herself, all stiff-backed and proper. He'd much rather have her ranting at him with that green fire in her eyes. He'd much rather be kissing her again.

"Are you going to eat?" he asked, hurt by the way she kept staring at the food.

"I'm not very hungry."

Letting out a breath, Rock grabbed her by the arms. "Ana, sit down, please. I need to...explain."

She looked at him then, her eyes full of doubt. "You don't need to explain, Rock. I understand things now."

"Oh, really?"

"Yes. I've felt it, seen it in your eyes. You disapprove of me. But you have to finish the work at my tea room. I only hope you can tolerate me enough to do the job."

"I'd never leave a job unfinished," he said, affronted that she'd even suggest such a thing.

"But you don't approve of me, do you?"

"Ana, sit."

She slumped onto the blanket, pushed at the sleeves of the big robe, then stared up at him.

Rock settled down beside her, his gaze moving to the fire. "When I was growing up, my mother was always working. We missed out on a lot of home-cooked meals and time together as a family because her art always took precedence over anything or anyone else."

Ana sat very still, staring at him. "Do you think I'm like that? Because I own a business and deal in art?"

"I don't know," he said honestly. "I only know that my behavior today, my attitude toward you and what you're trying to do, has been clouded by

these things I'm holding over from my childhood.''

"I'm not like that, Rock," she said, her voice
going soft. She looked into the fire, then said,
"Can I tell you something?"

"Of course."

Picking at some fuzz on the sleeve of his robe,
she said, "My sister Tara is the career woman.
She's the go-getter, the assertive, modern female.
Me, I'm the one who'd rather stay home on a Friday night, reading a romance novel and baking
cookies. I always wanted a home and a family, and
maybe a career on the side." She stopped, lowered
her eyes. "Once, long ago, I actually believed I
was close to having those things."

"What happened?" he asked, wishing he could
take the hurt out of her eyes. Wishing that he
hadn't added to that hurt.

"The man I'd dated all through college dumped
me for another woman."

"Oh." Rock hadn't thought he could feel any
worse about how he'd acted, but now he did.
"That must have been rough."

"It was," she replied, her eyes wide. "So I gave
up—on myself, on men, on having the things I
dreamed about. After college, I poured myself into
my work at the art gallery, but the whole time, I
held out hope for some sort of…release. Something that would fill the empty place in my heart."

She turned to him, pulling the robe tight against her throat as she sighed. "Since most of my relationships in the dating department didn't work out, I came up with this plan to own my own business. To be able to cook and be with people—two things I needed in my life to fill the emptiness. I decided if I couldn't have a family, I'd bring families together at least, and share their joy—you know, birthday parties, anniversaries, weddings, births, just getting together with friends. That's why I'm opening the tea room. I'm combining my love of cooking with my appreciation for art. It's that simple."

"Not so simple," Rock said, understanding dawning in his thick skull. "Ana, I know you've worked very hard to make this happen, but I didn't know what was behind it. And I'm sorry if I implied—"

"You have implied that you don't approve of women in business, women who have careers. I can't speak for your mother, Rock, but I can say this in my own defense—if I am ever blessed with a family of my own, nothing and no one will ever come between that family and me. I'd gladly cook meals three times a day, if only I had someone to share those meals with. But that doesn't mean I can't have a career. It's all about keeping your priorities straight, I guess."

Rock looked down at her folded hands against

the heavy terry cloth of his faded blue robe. Once, when the robe was new, it had held tiny bright sailboat designs. Now those designs were pale and washed out.

And that's how he felt now. Pale and washed out, so out of sync with the real world that he'd forgotten how a single woman might need a life and a career.

"Goodness, when did I become so judgmental?" he said out loud, his eyes still on those small, feminine hands clutching his old robe.

Ana lifted one of those hands to touch his arm. "Rock, have you talked to Eloise about this?"

He nodded. "Oh, yeah. We've talked for hours on end. She's trying so hard now to make amends. You know, she's always had a strong faith, but somewhere back there after our daddy died, she got lost. Her work was her salvation then. Now, she's reaping the rewards of that hard work, but she's also suffering the consequences, too."

"Is that why Stone is so bitter?"

"Oh, yeah. That and his love of money and power."

"You're bitter, too, no matter how much you try to deny it."

He grinned then, sheepish and red-faced. "Gee, you think?"

Ana leaned close, her smile as warm as the nearby fire. "I think you're struggling with this. I think you're trying. I only ask that you don't put me in the position of having to defend myself, because my choices have nothing to do with your issues with your mother.''

"You're right. I'm sorry I did that." He turned to reach for the tray. "Can we become friends again, over these lovely sandwiches I made?"

She nodded, reached for a half. "I think I'm hungry now." After nibbling for a while, she asked, "So if Eloise didn't cook, who did?"

"Me," he said, the silence of the one word speaking volumes in his weary mind.

His confession must have done something to Ana's resolve, too. Either that, or she was pitying him. She dropped her sandwich and took his hand in hers. "Rock, now that we've settled this between us, I want you to know that I'd be happy to cook you a meal anytime."

He pulled his hand away. "Don't feel sorry for me, Ana. I can take anything but that. We survived, me and Stone and Clay. And our mother wasn't a bad mother—she just got distracted by grief and…the need to create something that was solely hers." He stared down at the checkered blanket, wishing he hadn't revealed so much to her. "Let's just drop it, okay."

"Okay." She got up, her sandwich unfinished. "I'm going to get my dress and change. Where did you hang it?"

Rock could see the set of her shoulders. This tension between them wasn't going to go away over a haphazard picnic by the fire. He'd messed up all the way around.

But then things got even worse.

"I put it in the dryer."

Ana spun toward him, her eyes wide. "The dryer? Rock, that dress is rayon and dry-clean only. The dryer will shrink it."

Rock felt a sinking sensation moving from his shoulders to his stomach. "I'll go check. It's only been in there—" he glanced at the clock and groaned "—over an hour."

Ana ran a hand through her curls. "Just go get the dress, please."

He did as he was told. But when he pulled the hot dress out of the dryer, he could tell it wasn't exactly the same size and shape as it had been going in. What had once been a pretty, flowing white sundress sprinkled with blue flowers, was now a short, misshaped sheath with faded, wilted flowers.

With a sigh as heated as the dress, Rock emerged from the tiny laundry room off the back porch. "Here," he said on a low voice. "I...I think I ruined it."

Ana took one look at the dress and gasped. "Oh, oh—"

"I'll buy you another one," he said, his hands flying in the air. "Just tell me where you got it."

"It doesn't matter," she said, her voice calm in spite of the fire in her eyes. "I...just want this day to end."

"Well, so do I."

"Good. I'm going to try and get back into this so I can get home."

"I can loan you a shirt."

"No, thanks."

"Ana, I didn't mean—"

"I know," she said, her cheeks red. "You didn't mean to insult me, or judge me or ruin my dress. I know, and I understand. Let's just stick to business from now on, okay. No more meals together, no more pretense of anything other than a working relationship."

Her words stung Rock, but they also brought him back to reality. It was like being knocked down by a strong current. "Yes, ma'am," he said with a salute.

Then he cleaned up the leftovers of their meal and stalked to the kitchen. He didn't glance around when he heard the front door slam.

But he couldn't resist hurrying to the window to look for Ana's departing back. She had the dress on, but it was inches shorter and tight in all the wrong places.

In spite of that, in spite of how mad she made

him, in spite of her being so upset over a dress, in spite of all their differences and all the baggage he'd laid at her feet today, Rock decided she looked good walking away. Really good.

And he really wanted her to turn around and come back.

She'd look even better walking toward him.

Chapter Seven

Ana got up in a foul mood on Monday morning. It went from bad to worse when she saw the catty caption in the society section of the paper, under Greta Epperson's byline: "Preacher Dempsey Shares Intimate Lunch with the Lovely and mysterious Tea Room Lady."

Mysterious! The story went on to say that Greta had it on very good authority that the two were an "item."

"Ugh!" Ana threw the paper down, refusing to read the rest of the "story." If only Greta knew the truth! Not that it would probably matter.

Wishing she had someone to talk to, Ana remembered that Jackie and Tina wouldn't be in this morning. Ana had sent them and the rest of the newly hired waitstaff into Savannah to a training seminar on customer service. Thinking that in the mood she was in, she probably could have used some coaching in the "nice" department herself, Ana groaned and tried to concentrate on the computer screen.

Ignoring the hammering in the kitchen, she had come straight to her office. She'd have to forgo coffee, but it would be worth it if she could avoid seeing Rock. She was glad now that she'd given him a key so he could come and go at will while working here—but she knew he'd been here since dawn. She'd *heard* him loud and clear over the pounding inside her head.

His two helpers—that nice fellow Don and his shy, lanky son Cal—had gone off to buy more supplies. Last she'd heard, they'd be working at the shop today on various projects.

Which left Rock alone here with her.

Thinking back on the disastrous lunch they'd shared yesterday, Ana wished she hadn't gotten so mad about the dress. It was replaceable, after all. And it wasn't as if she'd paid a fortune for it. She'd bought it on a clearance rack at her favorite boutique. But…it wasn't the dress, really. It was more the way Rock seemed to take charge and just…assume things. Like, that she would willingly cook for him. Or that he knew how to handle a delicate dress better than she did. She supposed that kind of dominant attitude came from his being a bachelor. He seemed self-sufficient and capable and sure, as if he didn't really need anyone, except a cook. Why didn't the man just hire someone, then?

Oh, what did it matter, anyway? They were just as doomed as that lunch had been. *We have to cool things between us,* Ana decided. No more dinners by the bay, no more strolls on the beach, no trysts at the Wedding Rock, and especially, no more kisses. She wouldn't want dear, inquisitive Greta to get hold of that juicy bit of news.

She had to concentrate on getting this tea room off the ground. She couldn't let Tara down and she certainly didn't want to disappoint herself, either. So she pored over some order sheets, ignoring the overly loud commotion of hammer and drill in the next room, until the lack of caffeine induced a withdrawal headache and she was forced to walk across the hallway into the kitchen.

Which she immediately wished she hadn't done.

The sight of Rock standing there in a faded black T-shirt and old jeans, with his tool belt slung low over his hips, only reminded her of what a good-looking man he was. And that he'd kissed her twice the day before.

Ana took in a breath as she remembered those kisses. This man had made her a picnic in the middle of a rainstorm. That had been so incredibly sweet that she had thought she'd burst from sheer joy. But it had also shocked her.

She didn't know what Rock expected from her.

Then, he'd ruined her dress. That wasn't the real issue, of course, but it sure had been a good excuse to run away as fast as she could—in the shrunken, too-tight dress, at that.

Coffee, she reminded herself. The planked floor, treacherous and rude, squeaked and moaned when she tried to sneak on tiptoe to the coffeemaker.

Rock turned from studying his cabinet plans, his gaze slamming into hers. "Oh, hi," he said, wary. "I made coffee."

"So I see." Ana beat a path straight to the pot, then poured herself a generous cup. Grabbing a big oatmeal cookie from the batch she'd made last week, she took a moment to savor the quick breakfast.

"I had a cookie, too," Rock admitted, one bronze-toned hand resting on the butcher-block work island.

"Help yourself."

"Thanks." He shifted, waved a hand toward the cabinets. "Almost done with the main wall. I'll probably be ready to install the pantry doors and the rest of the bottom units by the end of the week. And Don's going to get the island installed later today."

"That's good."

He glanced up at her. "Do you...I mean, are you satisfied?"

Shocked, Ana frowned, almost choking on a bite of cookie as she glared at him. "What do you mean?"

"About the cabinets?" He shoved at blueprints and loose nails. "Do you like what I've done with the cabinets?"

"Oh, yes. I do." She bobbed her head, flushing over her misunderstanding. "They look great. Wonderful. Perfect."

With that, she pivoted to make a hasty exit.

"Ana?"

She didn't dare look back. "Hmm?"

"Can we be friends again?"

Ana stared at a dark spot on the wood casing of the doorway, wondering how the spot had come to be there. She rubbed a finger over the aged wood. "We are friends, Rock. As well as business associates."

"Well, do you have to be so business-like?"

She turned back then, to find him standing there with his hands on his hips, all male, his presence filling the room with suppressed tension. Ana's headache beat against her brain in the same way Rock had steadily been hammering the cabinets. "How do you want me to be?"

"What kind of question is that?"

She shrugged. "I'm just trying to get through this, Rock."

He slammed his hammer down, jarring the counter. "See, that's exactly what I mean. You aren't smiling. You aren't fussing and fixing. You're just…standing there."

"I only came in here to get a snack," she said, holding up her favorite sunflower coffee cup. "Sorry I disturbed you."

"You're not disturbing me," he replied after a long-winded sigh.

"Okay, then maybe we should both get back to work."

"Ana."

He said her name as if it were something precious and rare. It sent shivers through her system.

"I'm sorry, Ana."

"If you're talking about the dress, forget it. It was old, anyway."

"It's more than your dress, and you know it," he said.

He'd somehow gotten closer. She knew this without turning around. Ana kept her eyes on the office door across the hall, ready to bolt if he tried to touch her. "I need to get back to work. I have to pick up the girls at the airport in Savannah later today."

"Want me to go with you?"

"No, thanks. I just need you to keep working on those cabinets."

"Oh, I see. Is that how it is now? Just get the job done and get out of here?"

"I didn't say that."

He moved away. Ana felt the cool breeze of him turning, even before she heard his stomping work boots.

"There's a lot not being said between us, but maybe you're right. I have a job to do, and you have other obligations."

"That's right. Best to remember that."

"Yeah."

He picked up his hammer and proceeded to knock a nail against wood. With force.

Good, Ana thought. That meant he'd be done soon.

So she could get back to matters at hand. Like her tea room and her nieces.

And her sad, empty life.

Rock finished the glass of iced tea, then set the empty plastic cup down on the porch. It was late afternoon and he was tired. He'd put in a full day at Ana's house, but he'd gotten a lot done. Another week or so, and her kitchen would be completely renovated.

He only wished he could mend this rift between them with glue and nails. Their bond seemed permanently broken. No more kisses or fights. Just civility and long, uncomfortable bouts of utter silence. It made him think of a quote by Thomas Mann: "Speech is civilization itself.... It is silence which isolates."

"You can say that again, buddy," Rock whispered.

He looked over at Miss McPherson's porch. Milly sat there in her favorite rocking chair, steadily rocking as she stared out at the sea. Deciding he needed a friend—and maybe a bowl of stew—Rock hopped off his porch to stroll over to his neighbor.

"Evening, Miss Milly."

"Evening, Rock."

"How are you tonight?"

"I'm dandy. Your stew's in the freezer."

Grimacing at his own transparency and Miss McPherson's keen awareness, Rock sputtered and stammered. "Uh, well, thanks."

Milly kept rocking, her beaded eyes on the crashing waves down the beach. "What's eating at you, anyhow?"

"Me?" Rock asked, glancing around as if someone were behind him.

"Don't see anyone else lurking about my porch."

Settling down on the wide steps of her tiny cottage, Rock stared up at his old friend. "Milly, how come you never married?"

Milly stopped rocking. "What a strange question."

"Rude?"

"That, too."

"Well, I'd just like to know."

"Think you might be headed into permanent bachelorhood? Maybe you'll wind up rocking on your porch, too?"

"Something like that."

"Have a fight with your sweetheart?"

"She's not my sweetheart."

Milly placed her hands on the arms of her rocker and eyed him. "Yes, she is."

"What makes you say that?"

"Well, everyone is talking about it. I just read in Greta's column—"

"Forget that nosy woman. What makes *you* believe that Ana and I are...close."

"Goodness, it doesn't take a news flash to see it's the truth," Milly replied. "Over the past week or so, you seemed spry and happy. Now you look so hangdog, is all."

Wincing at being called spry and hangdog in the same breath, Rock nodded. "I made a mess of things with her, that's for sure."

"Such as?"

Rock told Milly McPherson the sad tale of his

rainy Sunday afternoon with Ana. "I ruined her pretty dress to boot."

"I did like that dress," Milly said, her lips pursed. "You know, I'm still pretty handy with a needle and thread."

"That won't fix this dress, Milly."

Milly leaned down, a conspiring tone in her exaggerated whisper. "You find me some pretty cotton or linen and I'll whip up another dress for your sweetheart."

"You could do that?"

"My eyesight certainly isn't what it used to be, but I reckon so."

"But…what about her size?"

"I have a good eye for that still. I'd say about a size six."

"She is slender. But womanly, too. And she did look pretty in that white—" Rock stopped when he realized Milly was watching him with those overly observant, aged eyes. "Oh, whatever you think you can do. I'll pay you to make the thing."

"Won't be necessary."

"But—"

Milly pushed up out of her chair, taking her time to stand straight. "But nothing. We'll set things right between the two of you."

"You are a kind and dear friend."

"Stop trying to sweet-talk me. Just go in and get your stew. I'm going to watch *Jeopardy*."

"Okay." Rock got up to go to the freezer that Milly kept in a shed off the garage.

"My suitor never returned from the sea," Milly said, one hand on the screen door, her back straight.

"What?"

"You asked why I never married," she said, her tone firm and controlled. "The man I planned to marry was killed out there. It's been near sixty years." She waved a hand toward the vast ocean. "Same as your daddy—working on the boats. Storm got him."

"I never knew," Rock said, a certain sadness falling over the twilight around him.

"We don't talk of such things," Milly replied. Then she went into the house and shut the door.

Rock stood there in the gathering dusk, with the sound of the swirling ocean behind him, and the moon and the stars beaming down on him from above. He wished for something he couldn't see or touch. And he knew it was there, waiting for him, just out of his reach.

Ana reached the airport in Savannah in record time, considering the rush-hour traffic, and considering her headache had turned into some kind of monster in her head.

The tension headache increased with each thought of seeing her sister again. But that stress was much easier to handle than spending the day trying to avoid Rock.

He'd gone out for lunch. That much she knew. She'd seen the remains of his chicken box in the trash.

Ana refused to feel guilty about not catering to Rock, as she'd done the week before. But she'd tested most of her recipes three times over and the menu was being printed already. No need to get overzealous about showing off her cooking skills. Especially with Rock. She wouldn't want to give him the wrong idea.

He probably got the wrong idea when you kissed him yesterday, she reminded herself as she sped into the pick-up lane at the airport. Glancing at the curb, Ana pushed thoughts of Rock out of her mind while she swept her gaze over the emerging travelers.

Then she saw Tara and the girls and immediately felt a bittersweet tug inside her heart. "Tara," she called as she stepped out of the car. "I'm here."

"Hi." Tara Hanson Parnell looked like a fashion plate in her white capri pants and black sleeveless summer sweater, her long blond hair just dusting her bare, tanned shoulders. Her strappy black sandals and matching designer bag gave her the look of a world traveler. And made Ana feel downright dowdy in her denim jumper and T-shirt.

But Ana didn't care right now. Just the sight of her three nieces brought tears of happiness to her eyes. "Hello, girls," she called, as the three rushed to greet her.

They all started talking at once.

"Aunt Ana, Marybeth says I can't get in the ocean because of sharks."

"Laurel, would you keep your paws off my purse!"

"Amanda, give me my lip gloss back, right now."

Ana glanced from one exasperated teenager to the next, then looked over their scrawny shoulders to find their mother's frowning face.

"Laurel, please refrain from antagonizing your sisters," Tara said to her eldest daughter.

Laurel gave her mother an exaggerated shrug, shifted on her platforms and said, "Whatever," with a toss of her crimped hair.

Tara, in spite of being dressed to the hilt, looked haggard and tired up close. She dropped a silver-bangle-bracelet clad arm against her hip. "They have argued, fussed, snapped and whined for the last week. I don't know why I bothered taking them to Texas to see their grandparents. They hated the whole experience."

Ana hugged each girl, making sure each got equal measures of squeezing and kissing. "Didn't you girls have fun with the Parnells?"

Laurel, blond and hyper like her mother, and wearing a too-short shirt that revealed her belly button, nodded. "Oh, we love Grandma and Grandpa. But they live on a ranch and they don't have cable." She rolled her eyes in horror, then glared at her mother. "And Mom expected us to just sit there, staring at chickens and cows."

"Imagine life without cable television," Ana said, shaking her head in mock concern.

"It was pretty bad, Aunt Ana," Marybeth said, tossing her golden-brown hair over her shoulder. "No movies or MTV."

"You aren't even allowed to watch MTV," Amanda piped in.

"Well, neither are you, but you sneak," Marybeth replied, sticking out her tongue.

"Do not."

"Do, too."

"Hush up, both of you," Tara said. "Now get in the car before your aunt gets a ticket."

Still catty and vocal, the girls piled in the back seat in a tangle of legs and platform shoes, while Tara and Ana finished putting their many bags into the trunk.

Tara tipped the skycap, then slid in the front beside Ana. "Thanks. This trip was tough. The Parnells are still so sad over Chad's death. They cried when the girls started packing up to leave. Then they cried again at the airport."

"How'd you hold up?" Ana asked, tears pricking her own eyes.

"I did okay." Tara stopped, took a breath. "I...I felt as if Chad's folks would somehow blame me...you know, for his death. But they were really sweet. Just a bit overprotective, given the circumstances. I did promise to let the girls come back soon." She sniffed, sighed again. "Anyway, thanks so much for...everything."

"You're welcome." Ana concentrated on getting out of the pick-up lane and back into the flow of traffic leaving the busy airport. Deciding to lighten the mood, she asked, "So...I have these three *adorable* ragamuffins for the entire summer?"

Tara smiled tiredly. "I know, I know. It strikes terror in your heart, right? I went through three nannies in as many weeks before we left for Texas. And once we got there, I knew right away the Parnells wouldn't be able to handle the girls for very long. Like I said, they were very sweet about everything, but they're old and get ornery at times, and they're still grieving about Chad's death. It was awkward, seeing them again, and even though they would have insisted on my leaving the girls there, I didn't dare ask them to help out. Plus, I couldn't bear to be that far from the girls all summer. And since Mom and Dad are traveling somewhere in Maine in that trailer-thing of theirs, you were my last hope. I was desperate, Ana.''

''Must have been, to ask me to do this right in the middle of opening my tea room.''

Tara pushed thick blond hair off her face, then popped her black wayfarers over her blue eyes. ''You can still back out.''

''I'm teasing,'' Ana said, acutely aware of her sister's somber mood. Tara was usually bubbly and edgy, always on the move. But now she slumped into the seat and stared straight ahead. Worried, Ana added, ''Hey, you know I love the girls. And you did say you'd drive out on the weekends. They'll be safe here.''

''I know,'' Tara said. ''It's just that...'' She stopped, swallowed. ''I just really need them to be with someone I can trust right now. I've got so much work to do, and I worry about them. It hasn't been easy, these past few months.''

''I understand,'' Ana said, wondering what, besides grief over Chad's death, was wrong with her sister. Tara never let anything get her down. She loved her three daughters to distraction. And since their father had died too young from a heart defect and too much stress, she supposed Tara was having anxiety attacks over the well-being of her children, just as the Parnells had probably done.

But then, they'd all been affected by Chad's

death. Ana figured she herself would have to deal with that sooner or later. It would have to be later.

But the hurtful memories seemed to surround her like the cars buzzing by. Chad and Tara had started their family right away. And Tara had been so young—just eighteen. Laurel was the firstborn, then a year later, Marybeth. Then two years later, Amanda.

The family I always wanted, Ana thought. *The family I should have had.*

The old resentment returned for just an instant. Ana squelched it, her smile reflecting in the rear-view mirror as she looked in the back seat at the squirming girls who resembled their father so much. She had long ago gotten over envying her sister.

But she'd probably never get over Tara's marrying the man Ana had once loved.

Chapter Eight

"I love it," Tara said, spinning around as she viewed the new tea room kitchen. They'd already toured the whole house. "Really, Ana, you've turned this old place into a showcase. You're going to be the talk of the island—and probably Savannah, too."

Ana shrugged. "I do hope to get tourists from Savannah and all over the state." Then she grinned. "Okay, all over the South would be good, too."

"You'll be a household name," Tara said, her lacquered nails drumming on the new island workstation that Rock and his two assistants had been working on for the past week. "Ana's Tea Room—it's the place for wedding showers, luncheons, or a quiet little lunch for two. Can't you just hear it?''

"Right now, I hear the sound of feet running around upstairs,'' Ana replied, glad that Tara approved of what she'd done, since her sister had co-signed the bank loan. "I'll order pizza for them tonight, then start them on healthier fare tomorrow.''

"Good luck with that,'' Tara said. "They only eat junk and then complain that they're too fat. Especially Laurel. She eats in spurts.''

"Typical teenager,'' Ana said, handing her sister a glass of mineral water. "Remember how we used to worry?''

"All through college, too,'' Tara said. Then, stopping, she gave Ana a flustered look before hastily adding, "But we still managed to eat a lot of pizza late at night.''

"Sure we did.'' Ana turned away. She wouldn't let Tara see the bitterness in her eyes. That time was over and Chad was gone to both of them now. No sense hurting her sister even more with re-hashed grudges. Tara would only be here a couple of days before heading off to get started on this real estate venture. Ana didn't want their time together to be awkward. "Anyway, the girls could use some meat on their bones. They look skinny to me.''

"They eat all the time,'' Tara replied, her tone

defensive in her words. "Of course, Laurel won't eat when she's in one of her pouty moods. Honestly, I hope you can bring her out of this horrible attitude she's had lately."

"I'll see what I can do to cheer her up," Ana said. "And how about you? You've lost more weight yourself."

"I'm always on the run, too busy and tired to eat a decent meal."

"Well, I'll have to remedy that while you're here, at least."

Ana knew Tara ate like a bird. She had to wonder if the girls hadn't noticed this and tried to emulate it. They were thin, but they seemed healthy. Her sister, on the other hand, looked pale and tired in spite of her expensive cosmetics.

Ana supposed being a widow did that to a person.

She dialed the pizza number, thinking the whole time that Chad Parnell hadn't stood a chance against Tara's beauty and charm. He'd loved Ana—she had to believe this. But one look at Tara and he'd been a goner. And in her heart, Ana knew that Tara and Chad had fit each other much better than she and Chad ever would have. Ana, always studious and just over a year older than her sister, had entered college at a young age and was graduating early. And because Ana had promised their parents she would watch out for her bubbly, outgoing sister, it made sense that she and Chad would tutor Tara. After a few weeks of the two seniors hovering over her freshman sister, Ana could sense Chad drifting away. Soon there were study sessions between Tara and Chad that didn't include Ana. She didn't even try to fight it. She just let him go. And yet, she'd loved him. Completely.

But she loved her sister, too. And forgiveness was much easier and safer than bitterness and anger. So all through the years, she'd kept her distance and kept her hurt and sense of betrayal to herself. After all, Tara hadn't really betrayed her. Tara had fought against her feelings for Chad, but in the end, love had won out.

After Chad had broken things off with Ana, Tara had confessed everything to Ana in a fit of tears, one long, cold winter night. And Ana had forgiven her and told her to follow her heart. Chad had never bothered to explain, except to say he was truly sorry.

Ana could still see them on their wedding day. How could she fault either of them for being so in love, for being so happy. Except when they glanced at her. She'd hated the guilt in their eyes as much as she'd hated the hint of betrayal she felt in her heart.

So she'd tried very hard to compensate for that guilt and for her emptiness through the years. She had tried to be a good sister, but since the marriage between Tara and Chad, things had always been strained. The girls coming along had helped there, though. Ana loved them so much, and tried to be a good aunt.

She'd keep on doing that now, too. She didn't want to lose Tara and the girls. She needed them as much as they needed her. Over the years, Ana had tried to reach out to Tara. They'd gotten much closer in recent years, and that closeness had gone one step farther when Ana told Tara about her dream to open a tea room. After that, Tara had insisted on helping Ana out financially. Then, just before Chad's death, they had finalized the loan.

Ana had to wonder if it were guilt-money, paid to soothe the stilted silence that sometimes flowed between them. But she'd accepted, thinking it would give Tara something to focus on, too. Which it had, since Chad's death.

"It's good to be here again," Tara said, bringing Ana back from her bittersweet thoughts. "Last time we got together, we were so wrapped up in setting up the contract and the construction for this place…well, it's been a while since we've had some downtime together."

"Not since the funeral," Ana said, after ordering two large veggie pizzas to be delivered. Then she turned to Tara. "How are you, really?"

"Honestly?" Tara asked, shaking her head.

"It's hard to say. I miss Chad, of course. But learning the business end of things these past six months is keeping me busy. And, of course, my own work is very necessary right now, too, just to help with the bills. This deal I'm working on in Atlanta, plus the sale of the land Chad left me near Savannah— well, if both go through I can at least relax about the girls' future."

Ana frowned. "I thought you were secure, money-wise. I mean, I thought Chad had plenty of life insurance and—" She stopped. "I don't mean to pry."

"It's all right," Tara said, waving a hand in the air. "It's complicated. You know, probate and litigation, things I'm only just beginning to understand. And some surprises I didn't even know about."

"But you're okay, right?"

"I'm fine, just fine," Tara replied, laughing. "Now, Miss Ana, I want to hear all about you. Who is this Rock you keep mentioning? The carpenter, right?"

Ana dropped her eyes. Had she really mentioned Rock that much in conversation? "Yes. He's Eloise Dempsey's son."

Tara's perfectly shaped brows lifted. "*The* Eloise Dempsey?"

"The only one around these parts," Ana replied. "I met her when we displayed some of her sculpture pieces and crosses at the gallery in Savannah. In fact, she's the one who told me this house was for sale. Said it would be perfect for my tea room, and she was right. I'm planning on showcasing some of her smaller pieces, and, hopefully, selling them, too.''

"That won't be a problem," Tara said. "Her work fetches top dollar among the A-list crowd. Those exquisite crosses she makes from old driftwood and stones are just beautiful.''

Ana nodded. "Well, anyway, Rock is her eldest son. And an artist in his own right, even though I wouldn't say that to his face. He's worked overtime to rebuild the entire kitchen. And he's still got some work left before the opening.''

"You're blushing," Tara said, grinning. "This has got to be good.''

"He's just someone I hired to built cabinets," Ana said, hating her own defensive tone.

"Uh-huh. A carpenter. A man who works with his hands.''

"He's also a preacher," Ana said, just to level things out in her sister's overactive mind.

"How very interesting.''

Ana couldn't help but laugh at Tara's wide-eyed smile. "He is interesting. Too interesting. And... he shrunk my favorite dress.''

Gasping, Tara grabbed Ana by the arm. "C'mon and sit down. You have to tell me *everything.*''

* * *

"Things are coming along nicely," Rock told his mother the next morning. "I've been working day and night on the cabinets for Ana's kitchen, while Don and Cal built the workstation off-site, then brought it in piece by piece to the kitchen. Honestly, Mother, you didn't call me this much when I left home and went off to college at Georgia Tech."

"Am I bothering you?" Eloise asked, the sweet Southern lilt of her voice carrying over the phone wire.

"No. More like…amusing me," Rock retorted, his coffee cup in midair. "I've doing a job for Ana and we're just friends. That's the story, regardless of what you might read in the papers."

"Really?"

"Really."

"Well, old Miss McPherson seems to think otherwise. Caught her in the five-and-dime the other day, buying some pretty white and blue sprigged linen fabric. Said she was going to make a dress for Ana—to replace the one you ruined."

"Miss McPherson is a good soul, and way too innocent to encounter you. My guess is that you badgered her for information."

"I did ask a few choice questions, yes."

"Well, stop asking. And please don't fuel Greta Epperson's fire, either. Milly agreed to sew Ana a dress, that's true. But it's only because I shrunk Ana's Sunday dress in the dryer.''

''And why would Ana's dress be in your dryer in the first place?''

Rock groaned, then set down his cup with such a *thud,* coffee splashed out on the counter. ''We got caught in a rainstorm after church. I brought her in to get out of the cold and wet.''

''And?''

''And…nothing. We had a quick lunch, then she left.''

And by the way, I kissed her. Twice. Really long, sweet, life-altering kisses. But that was after I'd insulted her and implied I needed her to cook for me.

Searching his mind for patience, Rock thought of the Proverbs: ''For the Lord giveth wisdom: out of his mouth cometh knowledge and understanding.''

Wisely, Rock refused to give her the details.

''Okay, all right,'' Eloise said, letting out a mother's frustrated sigh after a moment of silence. ''I have to get to work. Just wanted to check in.''

''I'm fine. Ana is fine.''

''You know, the lighthouse festival starts tomorrow. You could ask Ana to take a stroll with you.''

''I could, except she has her three nieces here.''

''Oh. Well, you'll find a way, I'm sure.''

"There is no *way,* Mother. Could we just drop it?"

"Of course. Oh, I heard from Clay. He might come home toward the end of the summer. Says he needs a vacation."

"Big-city cop beat getting to him?"

"Maybe. He wouldn't say. You know he never wants to worry us."

"No, never. Clay is very thoughtful that way."

"Are you being sarcastic?"

"No, I'm being honest. I appreciate that about my baby brother."

"As compared to your middle brother?"

"Maybe."

"I'm going to hang up now, before we get into a deep discussion about Stone."

"That's probably smart. See you later, Mom."

Rock headed out the door in a dark mood. He was still as mixed up about his feelings for Ana as a jellyfish caught in seaweed. He was highly attracted to the woman, but felt he should avoid her at all costs. But his argument about her being consumed by work was fast fading. Ana wasn't unnaturally obsessed by her tea room; she just needed to make a living, and, naturally, that required a lot of work and attention to detail. He couldn't fault her for that, yet he didn't want to get caught up in something he couldn't control. He'd just have to pray his way through this, because it would be hard to spend the day hammering nails if he couldn't stop this hammering doubt in his brain.

"He sure likes to hammer a lot," Marybeth whispered to Ana around high noon. "Does he ever take a break, Aunt Ana?"

"Rarely," Ana answered, remembering the first week of sweet camaraderie she'd shared here with Rock. That bond was now shattered. And Rock was working like a man on a mission. "He wants to get finished, honey. He's a very busy man."

"And cute, too," Laurel said on a sigh. "But not as cute as Cal. How old did you say he was?"

Ana hid her smile. "Rock? Oh, he's around thirty-four or -five, I think."

Laurel rolled her big baby blues. "I meant Cal! He looks so cool in his baggy shorts."

"Oh, Cal?" Ana gave her niece a mock glare. "He's seventeen."

"I'm almost fifteen," Laurel pointed out, grinning. "Maybe I can get to know him this summer."

Ana shook her head, thinking she was going to have to watch that one. Already blossoming, Laurel was just as pretty as Tara had been at her age, and all blond-haired and blue-eyed and boy crazy, just like her mother.

"Cal works a lot with Rock, honey. He might not have much free time."

"That's a shame. This is such a neat place. When can we go to the beach?"

Relieved that Laurel's fickle mind had drifted away from the subject of Cal Ashworth, Ana said, "Maybe later today."

Marybeth slumped onto the chair next to the desk. "Aunt Ana, we're so bored. Can you take us to the mall?"

"Mall?" Ana chuckled while she shifted some papers on her desk. "We don't have a mall, sugar. Just rows and rows of boutiques and souvenir shops."

"No mall?" Amanda bounced up off the small love seat nestled underneath a long window. "But…we have to have a mall!"

"She said no mall. Are you deaf?" Marybeth stuck out her tongue at her younger sister.

"Marybeth, sweetie, I'd really like to see that tongue back in your mouth. That's not very lady-like," Ana said, her smile belying her firm tone.

"She'll never be a lady," Amanda said, plopping back down against the fluffy pillows of the love seat. "She's a tomboy—reckless—that's what Mom says."

"Oh, I don't know about that," Ana said, glancing over at Marybeth. "I think pretty soon all of that will change."

"Just because I'm not afraid, doesn't make me

a tomboy,'' Marybeth retorted. ''I can do anything a boy does, except better.''

''A feminist, too,'' Ana said, laughing. ''No wonder your mother has her hands full.''

Laurel picked at the pens and papers on Ana's desk, then motioned toward her younger sisters. ''I think they're both dorks myself.''

''No name-calling allowed on these premises,'' Ana said.

''Okay, but I can still think it.''

''Hey, he's stopped hammering,'' Amanda said, springing up off the couch just in time to run smack into Rock as he entered the office.

''Whoa,'' Rock said, holding his hands on Amanda's shoulders to keep from knocking her down. ''Where's the fire?''

''Nowhere,'' Amanda said with a shy smile. ''Are you finished?''

''Just taking a lunch break,'' Rock said, his eyes moving over the three curious girls to Ana.

''Where's your help?'' Laurel asked, craning her head around Rock.

''The Ashworths?'' Rock asked, a perplexed expression on his face. ''They went to lunch.''

Laurel showed extreme disappointment. ''Pooh! I thought maybe Cal could tell me about the island, as in what's fun and what's not.''

Rock stared hard at the girl before sending Ana a profound look. ''I'm sure Cal would be glad to...tell you all about the local teen scene. He's usually right in the thick of things, beginning with our youth activities at church.''

"Church?" Laurel looked shocked. "Aunt Ana, you don't expect us to go to church, do you?"

"I most certainly do. And Rock is right. Cal is involved with the youth programs at Rock's church. He'd be an excellent guide in helping y'all to become part of that group."

"Great," Laurel replied, flipping her hair in irritation. "That sounds like loads of fun."

"Church can be fun," Rock said, his eyes on Ana. "Especially if you attend with someone you like and enjoy being around. It's all about... fellowship."

Ana felt the heat of his gaze and tried not to squirm against her heavy wooden office chair. "So...you headed out?"

"Actually," Rock said, his gaze moving over the girls, "I was thinking I'd take all of you to lunch. The lighthouse festival—officially called Save the West Island Lighthouse Summer Jam Session—is in full swing along the boardwalk. They've got arts-and-crafts booths, music, and food—hot dogs, shrimp po'boys, funnel cakes, cotton candy—"

Before he could finish, he had three excited teenagers jumping in circles around him.

"Cotton candy? I love cotton candy!"

"And funnel cakes, too."

"I want a hot dog," Laurel shouted over the chatter of her sisters. "And maybe I'll buy a bracelet or some earrings at one of those booths, since there's no other place to shop around here."

Ana couldn't help but laugh. "I guess that answers your question. Girls, want to tag along with Rock for lunch before we head out to the beach this afternoon?"

"Yes," Marybeth said, answering for her sisters smugly. "But you're coming, too, right?"

Ana looked up at Rock, wondering if she shouldn't just make some sort of excuse. But Tara wouldn't be back for hours—she had a business meeting in Savannah—and it probably wouldn't do to shove the girls off on Rock, since technically he was still a stranger to them.

"Will you come?" Rock asked, the softness of the question leaving Ana breathless and warm.

"Do I have a choice?"

"No," he said at the same time the girls did. Then he leaned close, too close, and whispered, "And besides, we have chaperones. I think we'll be safe, don't you?"

Ana wondered about that. She didn't think she'd ever be completely safe around Rock Dempsey. Not that he wasn't a gentleman or a kind, gracious man. But his kisses—she could still feel the imprint of his firm, wide lips moving over hers—were

dangerous. Even thinking about that was dangerous. Wanting to kiss him again meant she wasn't
safe from her own heart.

"What if Greta sees us and writes another em-
bellished exposé?" That seemed like a good excuse not to go, at least.

Rock must have seen her turmoil on her face.
"It's just lunch at a crowded festival," he said, his
smile full of a dare. "Even if Greta spots us, it's
for a very good cause, and...no rain predicted."

"Good," Ana replied, grabbing her straw tote
bag and nodding, though against her better judgment. "Girls, go wash up. Be downstairs and ready
to go in five minutes. We'll walk from here."

"Cool," Laurel shouted as she bolted up the
stairs.

The other two followed, chattering like fussing
seagulls about who got to wear which shoes.

"Adorable," Rock said as he walked with Ana
to the front door.

"Aren't they, though?"

She found it hard to look at him. She'd missed
him. She'd missed their laughing together, eating
together, just being friends as they got to know
each other. And she wondered what exactly she'd
been so mad about.

"So they'll be here...how long?"

She managed a chuckle. "About a month."

Then, just to tease him, she asked, "Is that fear I see in your eyes?"

Rock nodded. "I've never dealt with girls. Brothers, now that I can handle. But teenage girls, that's a whole different thing."

"And after you assured me that the whole island would help me with them."

"I will help you," he said, leaning close again as they waited at the bottom of the stairs. "I want to help you—that is, if you still want my help."

"I'll need all the help I can get."

"I'll take that as a yes, then."

Ana smelled him—the scent of sawdust and varnish mixed with the clean fresh scent of the sea that was in his aftershave. Trying to maintain her balance, she pushed at the balustrade at her back. Rock pushed closer.

"Nice dress," he said, his eyes sweeping over her.

"Thank you." She'd put on an old, floral sheath, thinking to get some work done. Not thinking to go to lunch with him. "It's old."

"But pretty. Burnished sunflowers to match your hair."

Ana knew he wanted to kiss her. And she knew she wanted to kiss him, too.

But the sound of flip-flops hitting wood snapped her out of that daydream. Her mind foggy with longing, she glanced up to find three inquisitive girls staring down from the upstairs landing.

"Ready?" she asked in a squeaky voice.

Laurel hopped down the stairs, a wide grin splitting her face. "Oh, yeah."

Ana knew that grin. It made her blush in spite of herself. "Then, let's go."

Marybeth and Amanda followed, giggling and whispering.

"This is bad," Ana said to Rock under her breath. "First your mother, then Greta and Miss Milly, and now the girls. The whole island is going to get the wrong idea about us."

"Would that be so terrible?" Rock asked. He wasn't joking. In fact, he seemed very serious.

But since she could never be sure of what he actually wanted or expected from her, Ana didn't know how to answer him.

She only knew that when she was around him, her heart did strange things and her head lost all logic. And she hadn't decided yet whether that was bad or good.

Chapter Nine

The smell of popcorn wafted along the air as Ana and the girls strolled through the closed-off Lady Street, the main thoroughfare that ran beside the boardwalk across the small island. A big red-and-white banner over the town square proclaimed The West Island Lighthouse Summer Jam Session and listed the dates. Off in the distance, an instrumental band played a lively tune.

All along the way, the Victorian-style shops and restaurants, once private dwellings but now commercial properties, had thrown their doors open to attract more customers. Huge stone flowerpots filled with red and pink hibiscus trees graced each doorway or porch stoop, while the white gazebo in the park boasted red and pink tea roses and creamy yellow and white Cherokee roses. The whole square, surrounded with moss-draped live oaks, vivid azaleas and crape myrtle, and sweet-smelling magnolias, looked festive and ready for spring. And down the sloping shoreline, past the protected sea oats and the planked boardwalk, the ocean glimmered in shades of blue and green, with sailboats, fancy yachts and tourists boats gracing the waters out past the breakers.

"This is awesome," Laurel said, her eyes scanning the crowd. No doubt she was looking for Cal Ashworth.

She'd spotted the father and son at one of the food booths, but had lost them in the crowd. Ana could tell Laurel was extremely interested in cute but shy Cal. Laughing to herself, Ana decided Laurel might be a bit too much for poor Cal. He was used to more sedate females.

"What are you smiling about?" Rock asked a few minutes later, as he handed her a soft drink and a grilled chicken sandwich from a nearby restaurant booth.

"Oh, nothing," Ana replied, enjoying the balmy gulf breeze and the gospel singers who had taken the stage. "Teenagers, life in general, everything."

"You look content."

"I guess I am." After finding an empty picnic table, they settled down with their sandwiches, while Ana kept a watchful eye on the girls, who'd all wanted hot dogs, French fries and funnel cakes. She glanced over at Rock as she nibbled her own French fries. "I've always wanted to live in a place like this—small, homey, slow-paced, and near the ocean. I haven't really had time to get out and explore the island, so this is nice."

"You work too hard."

She gave him a quick look, searching for censure in his eyes. Seeing none, she relaxed. "I don't have a choice right now. Once we get established, I'll settle into a routine. I've already hired two very capable assistants to help with hostessing. And I have three waitresses lined up."

"You have been busy," Rock said. "I've been so preoccupied with getting the kitchen in order, guess I haven't notice anyone else much. But I do run into Jackie and that cute little Tina now and again. The dynamic duo, those two."

"They are worth every penny of their salaries, that's for sure. They've smoothed out the menu plans and the table arrangements while I've done a lot of work over the phone," she said. "And I interviewed several people before I even called you. I'll start training them next week. It's one thing for me to cook while you're tearing away and hammering, but I don't want the kitchen too crowded until you're just about finished. Then a couple more weeks, and we're in business."

"I don't mind you cooking." He gave her a

sheepish grin. "Guess you probably noticed that, though."

"Maybe we'd better change the subject," she suggested, her grin belying her serious tone.

"Good idea." He took a long swallow of his soda. "Are you nervous?"

"Some. More anxious than nervous. I just hope this works."

"I think it will," he said, his smile warming her as much as the afternoon sun. "As you can see, this island gets very crowded during the peak summer months. And people are always hungry."

She laughed, thinking their conversations always led back to food in spite attempts to change the subject. "I'll serve a light breakfast—pastries, cookies and muffins, things such as that," she said. "Then my regular lunch and dinner menus. And on special occasions, catered private dinners."

"But you will have some nights free?"

"Yes, hopefully. That's why I hired Jackie as my assistant."

He leaned forward, his sandwich half-eaten. "I am hopeful. I hope to take you away from work on some of those free nights—a movie, dinner, dancing. I hope you and I are friends again, at least."

"Of course we're friends, Rock." She wondered if they would ever be anything but that, in spite of how the image of dancing in the moonlight with him made her feel. "And I'm sorry I got so mad about the dress."

"You were mad because I was acting like a buffoon."

She tilted her head at that. "That's a good word for it. But I wasn't exactly acting like a lady myself."

"You are every bit a lady." He turned serious then, and she knew he had something on his mind. "'And throughout all eternity, I forgive you, you forgive me.'"

"Did you just make that up?"

"No. I have to give credit to William Blake."

"The poet?"

"The very one. It's from 'Broken Love,' if I remember correctly."

"Do you always quote poetry to find your way back to a woman's heart?"

He sighed, took her hand in his. "I wish I knew the way to a woman's heart. I seem to put my foot in my mouth every time I step on the path."

"You're getting there," Ana said, admitting what she felt without any remorse, which surprised her. She wished she hadn't done so when his eyes turned as dark as a midnight ocean.

"Am I?"

"We're friends again." She gave him a saucy smile, then bit into another French fry. "And I've learned at least this much about you—the way to your heart is truly through your stomach.''

He lowered his head, then shot her a frown. ''Hey, am I really that bad?''

She tossed her hair off her face. ''No.'' Giving him a direct look, she said, ''I understand…how it was for you growing up. To you, food is comfort. It makes sense, as long as you don't confuse things…about me…about us, with all that angst from your past.''

''You don't mince words, do you.''

''I believe in being honest.''

''Brutally honest.''

''I can see the truth of the matter.'' She played with her paper napkin, almost fraying it in her attempt to find the right words. She'd always been able to spot the truth, which was why she'd known about Chad and Tara falling in love long before either of them had admitted it. She wanted to be straight with Rock, so there would be no misunderstandings or false expectations. ''Rock, I just want you and me to…understand each other. We both have obligations, things we have to get done—that's life. But I want us to be friends, and that means being honest, too.''

''Well, I'm glad for your friendship, at least.'' He another swallow of his drink. ''And I'm glad you plan on being around for a while.''

"I hope so." She stretched, tossed her head back to enjoy the sun. "This is a perfect day."

"The Lord brings them out sometimes, just to refresh us and give us new hope."

"Well, it's working." She glanced around, searching for the girls. "I guess I should get them to the beach, so I can tire them out early. Maybe then I'll get some work done later tonight."

Rock indicated with his head. "Looks like Laurel finally managed to corner Cal."

Ana saw the blonde hovering near the table where Cal and his father sat eating fried shrimp. Cal was smiling at something Laurel had said. "She is just like her mother," Ana said. "Too pretty and too full of attitude for her own good."

"Tara is lovely, from the glimpse I caught of her as she was leaving this morning," Rock replied. "But I like her older sister better."

Blushing, Ana looked over at him. "That's a first." Then she stopped, swallowed. "Actually, once a very long time ago, another man said almost the same thing to me. But…he soon changed his mind."

Rock sat studying her for a minute. "Want to tell me about it?"

Ana was about to tell him everything, when Marybeth and Amanda came bouncing up. "Can we go to the fair out on the boardwalk? Just to ride the roller coaster and the Ferris wheel maybe?"

"What about the beach?" Ana asked, glad for the interruption. It probably wouldn't be wise to tell Rock everything about her one great lost love. He might think she was self-pitying and shallow.

"We'll be back in a few minutes," Amanda said, twirling her hair in her fingers. "Please, Aunt Ana?"

"I can see I'm not going to get much work done this afternoon," Ana said. "Okay, here's the deal. You have one hour. I'm going to be around, right here near the booths, if you need me. Is Laurel going with you?"

Marybeth scoffed, then crossed her hands over her midsection. "She ditched us for that guy."

"You mean Cal Ashworth?"

"Yeah, that boy she's gone all gaga over."

Ana looked around, then saw Laurel sitting next to Cal. Mr. Ashworth was nowhere in sight. "I think your sister should go with you, to keep an eye on you two." And so Ana could keep an eye on boy-crazy Laurel.

"We're not babies," Amanda drawled.

"I know that, but you're still too young to be wandering around among strangers all by yourselves."

"Why don't *we* take them, and Laurel, too?" Rock suggested, getting to his feet. "C'mon, Ana, we haven't had an afternoon off in weeks."

"But—"

"C'mon, Aunt Ana. You can ride the roller coaster with us."

"Oh, no."

"Aunt Ana," Rock mimicked, grabbing her hand, "it'll be fun. You need to have some fun."

"But what about all that work?"

"It'll be there when you get back. And I'll work extra hours tonight to make up for my time."

"I think I'm outnumbered here," Ana said. "Well, let's go get Laurel."

"I'll tell her to c'mon." Marybeth hurried ahead of them, obviously relishing being able to boss her older sister for once.

Rock took Ana by the arm, strolling with her toward the table where Laurel and Cal sat. "Young love. Sure does the heart good."

"You," Ana said, giving him a mock nasty glare, "are certainly no help. I can't run a business if you talk me into taking afternoons off."

"Good for the soul," Rock explained.

"But I thought you believed in working Monday through Friday, and playing only after working hours."

"I've been wrong before. I think I might be wrong on that account, too. Today is definitely a 'Let's play hooky day.'"

"I'm just not sure—"

"Do you want me to take the girls, so you can get some work done?"

Sensing the hint of frustration in his tone, Ana shook her head. "No. You're right. I deserve to spend some time with my nieces. But only for today."

He seemed content with that, but Ana once again got the impression that Rock was aggravated with her. If he was going to close up like a turtle and pout every time she mentioned work, then they did indeed have a problem.

Rock Dempsey could either accept her as she was, or he could just forget being her friend.

That thought troubled Ana more than she cared to admit. She wanted to be Rock's friend. She wanted to be with Rock, maybe as more than just a friend. But she also wanted his approval. If he couldn't give her that, then they would never see eye to eye.

Their day together was ending much too soon for Rock. The girls had enjoyed riding all the attractions at the small carnival that had come to town as part of the festival. They'd shared cotton candy and too many other sugary concoctions, and now they were ready to head down to the beach for the couple of hours before sunset.

Rock wanted to go with them.

He looked up as they were making their way back along Lady Street, to find his mother sitting in a wicker chair in front of a booth featuring some of her smaller designs.

"Rock!" Eloise waved, her beaming smile making Rock feel guilty. Hadn't he insisted to his mother that Ana and he were just *working* together? Yet here they were, in broad daylight, playing together, and for all the world to see, at that. There would be more coy comments in Greta Epperson's society column, he just bet.

Well, let them all stew. What he did was his business, as long as he held his moral ground. And Rock certainly had every intention of staying friendly and professional. As long as he didn't think about how much fun it was to kiss Ana.

His mother didn't miss any of it. As if reading his very thoughts, she asked, "Rock, what are you doing here? And Ana, too." The pleased-as-punch look she shot him made Rock groan inwardly.

"We just came to eat lunch," he said, the defensive squeak in his words ringing in the air.

"It's four in the afternoon, son."

"Is it? Wow, must have lost track of the time."

"We were only going to tour the carnival for an hour," Ana said, shaking her head.

Eloise frowned at her son, then smiled at Ana. "How are you, darling?"

"I'm good," Ana replied, her gaze straying to the pottery and ironwork displayed in the booth. "How's business?"

"I've done a fair amount," Eloise said, waving a hand at another woman who was manning the booth. "Lou here keeps track of the money, while I try to woo the onlookers and window-shoppers."

"I'd imagine people are clamoring for one of those crosses," Ana said, her hand moving over a pewter nautical-inspired cross about six inches in diameter.

"People were lined up earlier," Lou said from her spot inside the booth. "It was so gracious of Eloise to donate some of her art for the lighthouse cause."

"Glad to do it," Eloise said as she got up to straighten some of the hanging crosses, her long lime-green linen jumper falling to her ankles. "We all want to see the lighthouse restored. It's been a part of this island for over two centuries."

"Where is the lighthouse?" Laurel asked. She'd pouted for most of the afternoon, after Rock had pulled her away from Cal. But she'd wound up having fun with her sisters in spite of herself.

Eloise looked over at her, giving her a sharp appraisal. "It's on the other end of the island, near Hidden Hill. And who are you?"

Ana waved a hand at the three curious girls. "These are my nieces, Eloise. Laurel, Marybeth and Amanda Parnell. They'll be spending part of the summer with me while their mother works in Savannah."

"Charming," Eloise said, smiling at the girls.

"What's Hidden Hill?" Amanda asked shyly.

"It's a big old stone house, almost like a castle," Eloise said. "It belonged to the descendants of the first settlers on the island, and changed hands several times over the years, but now it belongs to my son, Stone."

"You have one son named Rock and one named Stone?" Marybeth giggled. "That's weird."

"And one named Clay," Eloise replied, her eyes on Rock as she spoke. "I'm a bit eccentric that way."

Trying to remain impassive, Rock said, "Our mother has a weird sense of humor, that's for sure. We actually have proper given names—which I won't reveal right now—but she nicknamed each of us after some of the things she uses in her art."

"Wow," Marybeth said, rolling her eyes. "Good thing she doesn't work with rock, paper and scissors."

Rock grimaced, then gently cuffed the girl's arm. "You are too smart for your own good. But it might be fun to antagonize my brothers by calling them Paper and Scissors."

"Do they live here?" Amanda asked.

"No," Eloise said, her eyes growing bright. "Stone lives out from Savannah, on a golf resort. He's a real estate developer—commercial properties mostly. And Clay lives in Atlanta in an apartment. He's a policeman—a K-9 cop, as he likes to put it.''

"Do they have children?'' Laurel asked, her curious eyes moving toward Rock, then her aunt, her smile encouraging.

"No, none of my boys are even married yet. But I remain constantly hopeful,'' Eloise said, her words pointed.

"Do they come and visit?'' Again, Laurel.

"Not as much as I'd like,'' Eloise replied, her eyes going dim for just a minute.

Rock shifted on his work boots, acutely aware of where this conservation might lead. "So you three are stuck with me—the carpenter/preacher/beach bum.''

Laurel laughed, then shrugged. "You aren't so bad, Rock.''

"Mr. Dempsey,'' Ana said.

"No, Rock is fine,'' he told the girl. "And thanks for the vote of confidence. I knew getting up my nerve to ride that roller coaster would pay off. You promised to come to Youth Group tomorrow night if I did, remember?''

"I remember,'' Laurel said, bouncing on her flip-flops. "And you promised Cal would be there, too.''

"I remember,'' Rock said.

"Cal Ashworth?'' Eloise perked up, a keen interest sparkling in her crystal eyes. "You know sweet Cal?"

"Laurel's got a crush on him," Marybeth gladly explained, her hands on her hips.

"I just like being able to talk to someone older and more mature, like me," Laurel retorted, her glare sending a warning to her sister. "We have the same interests."

That statement caused the other two girls to launch into a heated debate with Laurel about who exactly was the most mature among them, and just exactly what interests she shared with Cal.

"Hey, hey," Rock said, putting his hands together in a time-out signal at the girls' eye level, "you are all maturing in your own way and in God's own time. And Laurel's budding relationship with Cal is just that, nothing to get worked up about. Simmer down."

"Yeah, simmer down now," Laurel said, exaggerating her words to the point that they all started laughing.

Eloise quirked a brow. "I can see you and Ana will have your hands full this summer."

Rock understood perfectly the implications of that statement. Eloise was looping Ana and Rock together, as in dating, as in trying to control a family of flighty sisters.

A family.

The phrase hit Rock square in the gut, and with

an instant clarity that shimmered as brightly as one of his mother's polished crosses, he knew what had been missing in his life for so long.

He glanced up to find Eloise giving him a curious look, as if she, too, had just figured this out. He hated the hopefulness in her eyes, hated that she wanted him to be happy, when for so long he hadn't actually believed she cared.

Then he looked over at Ana. She stood in a wash of late-afternoon sunshine, her wild auburn hair burning with shards of gold and red, her vivid green eyes as pure and tranquil as a forest pool. She smiled at him, a perfect smile that spoke of contentment and peace, in spite of the chaos around them.

A smile that shattered Rock's own fragile peace and shifted the very earth beneath his feet, lending that same beautiful chaos to his confused soul.

He had finally fallen in love. But he couldn't be sure if he'd fallen for Ana, or just the illusion of what having a real family with Ana might be like.

Was this a beautiful, unattainable dream? Or could it be real, at last?

Rock glanced at the girls, still whispering and fussing, then his eyes locked with Ana's. She gave him a quizzical look. Could she see his feelings on his face?

Well, he had the whole summer to test this new,

disturbing theory of love. Trouble was, how was he going to keep his feelings a secret from Ana— who valued complete honesty above all things— until he could be sure?

Chapter Ten

"Hey, I found you."

At the sound of the shout, Ana turned from her spot on the blanket to find her sister strolling down the beach. "Hello," she called, waving.

Tara had changed into her swimsuit and a matching cover-up. She looked like a fashion model in her black straw hat and black-and-white bathing suit. Ana had opted for a floral bathing suit and cotton shorts to cover her thighs. And she had yet to get wet. She'd been too busy reading over the last-minute to-do lists and other paperwork she had to wade through before the tea room's opening.

"Look at that sunset," Tara said as she settled down beside Ana in a cloud of expensive perfume, her gaze moving off to the west behind the bay. "Where are the girls?"

"Beachcombing," Ana replied as she offered Tara a bottled water from a small ice chest. "I told them to stay close. They should be back soon."

Tara let out a long sigh, then lifted the top off the water bottle. "Boy, do I wish I could stay here a few more days. This feels so good."

Ana noticed the dark circles under her sister's vivid blue eyes. "How did your meeting go?"

"Okay," Tara said, her eyes scanning the ocean before she put her shades on. Then she shook her head. "If I ever get all the bank accounts and insurance policies sorted out, not to mention the stock options and 401K account, I'll be thrilled."

"Don't you have lawyers and accountants to handle all of that?"

Tara stared straight out into the water. "Yes, but I'm trying to do most of it on my own, just to familiarize myself with it." She sat silent for a minute, then said, "You know, Chad always handled the finances. Now I wish I'd paid more attention to the details. It's like moving through a never-ending maze."

"But you're okay, right?" Ana had a strange feeling in her stomach. Tara was being evasive. "Do you need me to help?"

Tara patted her hand. "You're helping already by letting the girls stay here. And I mean it, Ana—

make them work for their keep, the way Mom and Dad taught us to work. They can do odd jobs, wash dishes, help serve food.''

''I intend to keep them busy,'' Ana replied. ''But we did take the afternoon off, since it was their first day here.''

''That was thoughtful of you. So what did you do?''

Now it was Ana's turn to be evasive. ''Oh, we went to the lighthouse festival—ate junk food, then went on most of the rides at that little traveling carnival on the boardwalk.''

''Oh, I'm sure the girls loved that.''

''They had a blast,'' Ana replied, leaving out the part about being with Rock for most of the afternoon. It had been such a nice, peaceful outing, even with three noisy girls in tow. Rock had been a perfect gentleman, and they'd laughed and talked about little things. Ana had refrained from talking about work, however. She supposed that had been a good idea, since Rock seemed to enjoy himself, too. Remembering how he'd held her close when the Ferris wheel had stopped them right up on top, Ana had to smile.

''What's that smile all about?'' Tara asked, bringing her sunglasses down on her nose as she shot Ana a purposeful look. ''Must be a man involved, since you look so dreamy.''

''Not everything in life has to revolve around a

man,'' Ana retorted, sticking out her tongue in much the same fashion Marybeth often did.

Tara grinned, then tossed her hat down. ''Did Rock Dempsey just happen to tag along on this little excursion?''

''Oh, all right,'' Ana said, dropping her file of paperwork back in her tote bag. ''Yes, he did come along. The girls seem to behave better with him around. He has a soothing…countenance.''

Tara rolled her eyes. ''A soothing countenance? You make him sound like a nice old uncle.''

Lowering her head, Ana thought about that. ''He is nice, very nice. He's dependable, solid, hard-working. Not the type I'm used to, at all.''

''Not like Chad,'' Tara said, then instantly put a hand to her mouth. ''I'm sorry. That just slipped out.''

Ana thought about that. ''No, you're right. Chad was a bad-boy type. We both knew that. But he had a good heart.''

''Yes,'' Tara said, ''but that heart couldn't take all the stress of his demanding job.'' She grew silent again. ''Sometimes, I feel so guilty, as if I pushed him too hard.''

''You can't blame yourself, Tara. Who knew Chad had a heart condition? You can't predict things like that.''

Her sister took off her sunglasses and wiped at her eyes. ''I miss him so much. Chad had his faults, but I loved him in my own way. You have to know that, Ana.''

''I do,'' Ana said, painfully aware that even though Chad Parnell was dead, the issue of his having at one time loved both of them was still very much alive. Wanting to change the subject, she said, ''Now, let's get back to Rock. You need to help me figure him out.''

Tara gave a shaky laugh. ''Who can figure out men?''

''Well, you're right there,'' Ana agreed, lying down to soak up the last rays of the sun. ''But this one is different. I just don't know what makes him tick. He's old-fashioned and sweet, but I'm afraid those very things might get in the way of any kind of lasting relationship with him.''

''What do you mean?''

Ana shrugged, her bare shoulders brushing against the terry cloth of the seascape beach blanket. ''Rock's mother worked long hours when the boys were growing up. Being the eldest, Rock had to take care of his brothers a lot. Apparently, he cooked, cleaned, and worked odd jobs most of his teenage years. I think he still resents his mother because of that—''

''And therefore, resents working women in general?'' Tara asked, hitting the mark.

''I think so.'' Ana waved a hand in the air. ''At least, that's the impression I get. I think Rock wants a traditional kind of wife—someone who will cook, clean and provide an orderly house for him.''

''That *is* old-fashioned,'' Tara quipped, groaning. ''Funny, I tried to be that for Chad at first, but he didn't seem to notice. That's why I went into real estate. After the girls started school, I had to do something.''

Ana rolled to her stomach, then placed her head on her hands. ''This whole issue of a working woman—didn't we get over that in the last century?''

''You'd think.''

''But you know,'' Ana said, her mind replaying how much she'd enjoyed being with Rock, ''even if it's old-fashioned, I kinda like the idea of being a traditional wife. I like to cook and putter around the house. And I want a family.''

Tara shifted on the blanket, then stared down at her sister. ''You deserve that.'' She turned and watched the waves capping a few yards away. ''I took that from you, didn't I?''

Ana shot up. ''Let's not get into that, okay? Chad made his choice, and I accepted that.''

''You accepted *us*,'' Tara corrected. ''Ana, why didn't you ever scream and holler? Didn't you resent us?''

Ana thought long and hard before answering. ''Of course I did. But I love you, and I loved Chad.

Sometimes, because we do love so much, we also have to accept and let go. I was hurt, no doubt. But I love *you* more than I loved being bitter and hurt. I just couldn't see holding a grudge and losing my sister. We made it through."

"And now Chad is gone."

"But we have the girls."

"Yes, we do. And you are a wonderful aunt." Tara smiled then. "And an aunt who apparently is about to get a love life."

"I don't know about that," Ana said, falling back against the blanket, her eyes shut. "We'll have to see where things go with Rock."

"Hmm," Tara replied, slapping Ana on the arm. She was looking in the other direction. "I guess we'll soon find out about that. He's walking up the beach right now, with another fellow, a dog and…our girls."

Ana shot up again, her eyes scanning the horizon to the south. Behind them, the sun was setting in shades of orange and mauve. "What? Rock's here?"

"Don't hyperventilate," Tara said, swiping at Ana's back.

Ana spotted him then. He was dressed in cutoff khakis and an open, button-up shirt. He was laughing with the girls and…Cal Ashworth.

"That's Cal with him," Ana said. "Your eldest

daughter has taken an immediate liking to that young man.''

"Oh, great.'' Tara glared with a mother's intensity toward Cal. "Well, he *is* cute. But I think I might be the one to hyperventilate. Laurel and I have been at odds lately, maybe because she is beginning to notice boys. I can't stand the thought of my baby being old enough to date, and she can't stand the thought of me standing in her way.''

"Actually, she's really not quite old enough for anything serious,'' Ana said. "But they can at least hang out together. Cal comes from a good, Christian family.''

"So did Chad,'' Tara retorted. "Oops. Sorry again.''

Ana decided there was something going on with Tara. She'd made reference to Chad's shortcomings far too many times since his death. But now wasn't the time to bring that up.

Right now, Rock was walking toward her, a lazy grin on his face and a quizzical look in his eyes.

"Hello there,'' Rock said, hoping he looked nonchalant. He didn't want Ana to think he was stalking her. But his next words gave him away. "The girls said I'd find you here.''

"And how did you find the girls?'' Ana asked as she waved at him.

"They found me,'' he told her while he enjoyed

the view of her pretty legs underneath the baggy denim shorts. "Cal and I were finishing up some last-minute things at the shop when these three popped in."

"I saw the sign from the beach—Dempsey's Cabinetry," Laurel said, her chin jutting out in defiance. "So we walked over there." At her aunt's sharp look of disapproval, she added, "You said stay close. It's right up there." She pointed back over the hill toward the wind-tossed oak trees.

"And we found a dog," Marybeth said before Ana could protest any further.

"So I see. C'mere, boy." Tara squealed as the big, wet collie ran up and licked her face. Tara immediately began petting the animal, cooing to him in baby talk. "What a pretty boy, yes, he is."

"That's Sweetybaby," Cal said, his voice low and shy. "He's mine now. My mom's, actually— she gave him that dumb name." He shrugged. "My mom died three years ago."

"Oh, I'm sorry to hear that," Ana told the boy.

"Sweetybaby comes to the shop each day to fetch Cal home," Rock explained, changing the somber mood and hoping the friendly animal would win both Cal and him points with the womenfolk. "Somehow this dog just knows when it's quitting time."

"So why didn't you go on home?" Ana asked, a teasing light in her green eyes.

At least she seemed glad to see him. Rock relaxed. Over the past two hours, he hadn't been able to focus on work. And it was all Ana's fault. Since he'd realized right there on Lady Street that he might be falling for her, he'd wanted nothing more than to see her again. When the girls had shown up, he'd had the perfect excuse.

"We wanted him to come to the beach with us," Amanda told them in answer to Ana's question. Then she called to the dog. "C'mon, Sweetybaby, let's go play."

With that, the girls and Cal took off for the water, laughing and screaming as they tried to wet each other with the splashing surf.

Rock shrugged, then sat down on a corner of the big blanket. "I figured you'd be worried, so I told them we'd walk them back down here. And I made Cal call his sister so she'd know where he is, too."

"How very thoughtful," Tara said, her expression telling him that she didn't believe that paltry excuse. "But then, Ana has been going on and on about how thoughtful and kind you are, Rock."

Rock saw Ana lift a bare foot to kick her sister. "Has she, now?"

"I've been telling her all about *work*," Ana said. "About how you've worked overtime to make sure the kitchen is finished on time."

Rock felt the bubble in his heart deflating a little bit. "Ah, yes, we can't forget about that, can we?

Ana is on a mission to get things done, that's for sure.''

"She has to be," Tara replied. "Her livelihood depends on it."

Rock thought he'd heard the hint of a dare in her statement. Were these two formidable sisters ganging up on him and his old-fashioned notions?

"Nothing wrong with an honest day's work," he replied, hoping for damage control.

"Well, I'm glad we can all agree on that," Tara said, her smile serenity itself, while her blue eyes flashed a warning.

"Just ignore her," Ana said, giving her sister her own warning look. "Tara has always worked hard herself. She's a Realtor."

"So I've heard from the girls. Sounds as if you do pretty good at it, too."

"I make a living," Tara said. Then in a rush of hands and feet, she hopped up. "Think I'll take a dip before it gets too chilly out here."

She ran down the beach and straight into the water, her girls cheering her on while Sweetybaby tried to race after her in the waves.

"Was it something I said?" Rock asked Ana when they were alone. He didn't think her sister approved of him at all.

"No. She's just having a hard time since her husband died."

"It's only been a few months, right?"

She nodded, looked away for just a moment. "Chad was a good husband, but he worked day and night. He got caught up in his career, neglected his health. He was too young, way too young, to die."

"I'm sorry. That's tough, I know. I guess Tara is dealing with a lot, especially having to raise the girls on her own."

"We're all dealing with the situation. It was rough on Chad's parents, too. They're just not able to help with the girls."

"What about your parents? You don't mention them much."

She smiled, brushed sand off her leg. "They're fine. They like to travel in their new motorhome. They go to these get-togethers where everyone has a big, silver travel trailer. It's like a sea of little houses, all lined up."

"Sounds as if they're enjoying their retirement."

"They are. And they plan on coming through here later in the summer, to visit with the girls and help out some."

"Were they close to Chad?"

She gave him a panicked look. "Of course."

Ana got such a faraway look in her eyes each time he mentioned Chad Parnell. Maybe she was still dealing with his death, too. After all, from everything she'd told him, it appeared the Hansons were a close-knit family.

Feeling like an oaf, he decided to change the subject and try again. "You got some sun. It looks nice."

Ana glanced down at her skin. "Was I too pale before?"

"No, of course not. I just mean—"

He stopped, took a long breath. "I never know the right thing to say to you." He thought he saw pity in her eyes, followed by amusement.

"What?" she asked, giving him a measured look. "No words from a dead poet? No sage advice from a philosophy book? Not even a bit of wisdom from Proverbs?"

Okay, she *was* teasing him. He could take it. And he could give as good as he got, too. "How about I say it straight? You always look good to me, Ana. How's that?"

She actually blushed. "That's...just fine, Rock."

Then she jumped up and, running toward the ocean, tossed him a dare over her shoulder. "Bet you can't catch me."

Rock took that dare. "Oh, I intend to do just that," he said to himself as he hurried after her.

Chapter Eleven

❧

"It was nice of your mother to do this," Ana told Rock a couple of days later. It was late afternoon and they were on their way to Eloise's studio. She had invited the girls to come and see where she worked.

"And we'll let them explore their creativity," Eloise had said over the phone.

Rock turned up the winding tree-shaded drive to Eloise's big Victorian house. "I was surprised. My mother never lets anything or anyone get in the way of her work."

"Do you think we'll bother her?" Amanda asked from the back seat of Rock's utility van, where she sat squished between her sisters.

Rock glanced in the mirror to find Amanda's big

eyes on him. "Honey, she wouldn't have invited you if she didn't want you here."

Ana believed him. Rock was handling this with grace, but she still sensed the resentment in him. Obviously, he was trying to understand his mother, trying to stay close to her, in spite of what might have happened when he was younger. But then, Rock was that kind of man. A gentle soul who looked for the best in people. Rock nurtured the people who depended on him as a minister and a friend. He'd shown Ana so much about her own faith simply by talking to her and listening to her, then reassuring her. And he'd done this in spite of the rumors flying hot and heavy about their supposed love life.

But who nurtured and reassured Rock?

Don't go getting ideas, she told herself as she stayed safely in her corner of the car. It was bad enough that the whole island was involved in their personal lives, let alone her thinking they actually were more than just good friends. Still, she could be the friend he'd hoped for, if nothing else. That was a form of nurturing.

And the past few days had brought a tentative peace between them. It was a nice change—actually having the time to get to know a man before taking that next step. Perhaps that was where she'd gone wrong in all her relationships since Chad. She'd rushed things, hoping to find a perfect mate before her biological clock stopped ticking. With Rock, the slow and steady pace of getting acquainted had a very enticing rhythm. Ana prayed that she was on the right path, that she wasn't just imagining things. And she prayed that this sweet slow longing inside her heart promised something good and right.

But that slow rhythm doesn't allow for kissing him, she also reminded herself. When Rock kissed her, everything went into overdrive. Best to avoid those kisses and the feelings they provoked. Best to enjoy their friendship and the deep, abiding respect she felt for this man.

"This house is so cool," Marybeth shouted very near Ana's ear, deafening her into awareness.

"It belonged to my grandparents," Rock said as he pulled the van up underneath an aged magnolia tree.

"Do they live here, too?" Marybeth asked, opening the sliding door before the van had even stopped.

"No. They're dead now," Rock said. While the girls began piling out, he turned to Ana. "They were once the wealthiest people on the island, but when they got old, my grandfather had to sell most of their property. They wound up in a retirement home in Savannah. And that's where they died."

"That's sad," Ana said. "Why didn't they live here?"

Rock turned in the seat, waiting as Laurel took off her earphones and put away her CD player. After all the girls were out of the van, he said, "We never knew them. They disinherited my mother when she married my father. So we were never close."

Stunned, Ana looked up to find Eloise walking down a shell-covered path that ran from the main house to her studio. "Your mother gave up her inheritance for love?"

"Yeah. They had over fifteen happy years together before my father drowned. And…you know the rest."

Ana put a hand on his arm. "No, I don't know the rest. But I want to. Will you tell me about it sometime? All of it?"

"Sometime," he said, his eyes shuttered with darkness. Then he got out of the van and came around to her door before she could open it. "But not now."

Ana got out, her eyes on Rock as he greeted his mother. There was so much more to him, so many deep scars and troubling secrets hidden behind those wise eyes and that gentle smile. She wanted to know all of him.

She wanted to nurture him. That meant taking the step she'd been avoiding, that step that would take them beyond mere friendship. But it might be worth it this time. Because by doing so, she just might be able to heal her wounds, too.

Rock walked toward his waiting mother, wishing that he hadn't told Ana about his grandparents. But he hadn't told her everything. And maybe he never would.

But Ana wanted to know. Would she still look at him in the same way if she knew all about his hurts and his anger? He didn't want to lose the precious bond they'd formed.

And that was part of the reason he had brought Ana and the girls here today. Being with Ana made him a better man. It made him much more aware of his shortcomings, too.

"You're frowning," Eloise said as she reached to touch his face. His mother was a toucher. She liked to feel things, liked moving her fingers over the rough texture of life, hoping to carve the rough spots into something soft and beautiful. At least, she'd been working toward that with Rock.

Allowing her this small endearment, Rock formed the beginnings of a smile. "How's that? Better?"

"A little. You didn't mind bringing the girls, did you?"

"No, of course not." He watched as Laurel, Marybeth and Amanda glanced around the colorful, intriguing yard. "They came to conquer and explore."

"Welcome, girls," Eloise said, waving her arm in the air. "What do you think of my garden?"

Laurel shrugged. "It's weird."

Rock saw Ana cringe, but hurried to reassure her. "It's okay. She likes being weird, honestly."

"I told you, I prefer to be called eccentric," Eloise replied, her big silver hoop earrings jangling. "But these pieces are a bit different. Abstracts and modern art combined with some traditional pieces."

"I like the crosses on the tree," Amanda said timidly. "Could I make something like that?"

"Absolutely," Eloise told her. "I have plenty of scraps lying around. You can create whatever you want."

"I'm not good at art," Laurel said, sounding sullen. She was pouting because she'd wanted to go for a walk on the beach with Cal instead of coming to "make dumb artwork."

"You might just need to try something different, a new twist," Eloise said, her smile serene, her eyes taking in Laurel's stubborn stance. "You could make something special, to represent your stay on the island."

"Whatever." Laurel whirled to stare at a flower-shaped iron sculpture Eloise had created years ago. "That's cool."

"One of my first attempts," Eloise explained. "It's a lotus blossom."

"Looks like a rusty flower to me," Marybeth said. Then she put a hand to her mouth. "Sorry."

"Beauty is in the eye of the beholder," Rock said to his mother.

"And to each his own," Eloise retorted. "Now come girls. Let's see what else we can view and appreciate. We have to have art in our lives, to add human interpretation to the aesthetic beauty of God's world."

"She is weird," Marybeth whispered to Amanda. Ana shot the giggling girls a quieting glare, but they still managed to grin at each other and Rock.

Rock grinned back, then waited for Ana while the girls took off after Eloise. "I certainly see a beauty I appreciate," he whispered in Ana's ear as he glanced down at her.

"Beauty is in the eye of the beholder," Ana mimicked.

But she blushed as she said it.

"Let's go for a walk," Rock said much later.

The girls were safely ensconced in the high-ceilinged studio with Eloise. They were making things—small creations that they could give to their mother when she returned later in the week. Or keep for themselves, to store up and treasure.

The way Rock had stored up and treasured certain little baubles he'd made in his mother's studio whenever he'd been allowed a few quiet moments with her.

Ana stretched in the lounge chair where she'd been sitting. "Okay."

"Okay?"

"A walk?"

"Oh, right." He extended a hand to her and pulled her to her feet, the sweet smell of her floral perfume merging with the scent of magnolia from a nearby tree.

"You seem distracted," Ana said. "We could go on home."

"No, I'm fine. Just remembering."

"Want to tell me about it?"

They headed down the path toward the dunes, moonlight glistening against the sand in patterns of gray and blue. The sound of the whitecaps echoed up, calling to them in a serene melody. Rock prayed for some of that serenity.

"I have good memories," he said at last. "I don't want you to think I had a horrible childhood."

"I don't think that."

"I was just remembering once when I went out to my mother's studio late one night. She was standing there, bathed in lamplight, her hands moving and shaping a piece of clay. She looked so lovely, so at peace, her eyes flashing, her hands moving. Then she looked up at me, as if she'd known I was there.''

"Was she angry at being interrupted?"

"No, she invited me in and let me work on the sculpture. She told me there was a beauty in creating something just for yourself."

"What did you create?"

"An owl. I shaped the clay into an owl. I still have that owl sitting on my mantel."

"Your mother let you keep it?"

"Yes. She said it belonged to me now. I had touched it, shaped it, made it into something entirely my own."

"That's a nice story, Rock."

They were down on the sand now. They tossed off their shoes and walked barefoot toward the sea. "That's how I feel about us, Ana." He turned to her, his hands tentatively touching her soft curls. "I feel as if each time I'm with you, I'm molding and shaping something that can become mine. Does that make sense?"

He saw the fear, the doubt, reflected in her eyes. "Ana?"

"Do you want to mold me into something else, Rock?"

He pulled her close. "Goodness, no. That's not what I'm saying."

"Then, what exactly are you saying?"

He shifted, tugged her closer. "I'm saying I like being with you. I like what being with you does to me."

"But you want to own me?"

"No." He stepped back, ran a hand through his hair. "I'm saying...you're the one, Ana. You're the one who's changing and reshaping me. You're the one who's making me see that I've been sitting in judgment against my own mother."

He felt her hand on his arm. "I don't want to change you. I just want to understand you."

He put his arms around her again, savoring the warmth of her skin, the sweetness of holding her. "I'm not telling this...I'm not explaining it right," he said. With a groan, he urged her close, then lowered his mouth to hers.

The kiss held all of his dark secrets, all of his fears and worries. As his lips moved over hers, he felt those secrets and fears being shifted and sifted, like sand moving through water, into something full of light and hope.

"There," he said as he lifted his head and stepped back.

Ana stared up at him, her eyes wide, her lips thoroughly kissed. "There what?"

"There. I hope that explained what I'm trying to say."

"That only complicated things," she said, one

hand flying to her mouth. "I thought we'd decided to avoid…kissing."

"I never decided that." No, but he'd told himself a hundred times to stay away from her. From her tempting lips.

"Well, we agreed to be friends, to keep things more on a business level."

"This is a different kind of business. Personal business."

She kept staring up at him, her gaze transfixed in a wash of moonlight and night tides. "This… could ruin our friendship, you know."

"But that's what I'm trying to say. I think we might be on the verge of becoming more than friends. I don't know how to explain what you do to me, Ana."

She turned away, stared out at the water. "I can't be the woman you expect, Rock. I want my tea room."

Surprised, he felt as if she'd punched him in the stomach. "I don't want you to give up anything. I just want you to…keep doing what you're doing. To me."

"But you sound as if you're in some sort of pain."

He smiled, then tugged her around. "No. I mean, yes. It's painful to see one's own shortcomings, but it's also a good thing to find someone I enjoy being around. If it means I can be closer to you, then I'm willing to work my way through this.''

''So you're saying that even though it's torture to be around me, you like to suffer?'' she asked in a soft tone.

''Something like that.'' He stood silent, his eyes on her. Then he decided to fall back on his old ways for just a moment. '''Man cannot remake himself without suffering. He is both the marble and the sculptor.''

Ana didn't move, didn't respond.

''Alexis Carrel,'' he said. ''It's a quote.''

''I figured that out on my own,'' she replied.

''Well, I was just trying to explain.''

''So you're telling me you're suffering because of your feelings for me, but that's really a good thing because in the process, you're…changing… because of me?''

''Yes,'' he said, his hands waving in the air. ''Yes. I want to be a better man, so that you'll be happy with me, so that you'll want to be with me. And that means dropping some of my preconceived notions about women in general. It also means lots of prayer—*lots* of prayer.'' He stopped, inhaled. ''But it will be worth the price, worth the asking, worth the risk.''

''You're willing to take that risk…for me?''

He nodded, the revelation washing over him like

the ocean. And like those same crashing waters, it was both exhilarating and frightening.

"But that means you'd be doing all the changing, Rock," she said. "I don't necessarily want you to change. Not completely."

"I'd only change the stupid parts," he replied, hoping he wasn't scaring her away.

"And what about me? Don't I need to change some, too?"

"You're close to perfect," he blurted, then wished he hadn't said that. She looked up at him as if she didn't believe a word of it.

"Oh, no. I am far from perfect." She turned, stalked away, her feet slapping the sand. "Since college…since my heart was broken…I've searched for the *perfect* replacement. Someone I could love and have a family with."

Rock now understood the hesitancy in her, that quietness he'd seen and wondered about. She'd been in love before, he remembered. But she'd told him very little about that love or why her heart had been broken. Another revelation, but also another insight into Ana. "You thought you had that someone…in college?"

She looked out at the dark ocean. "Yes, but he fell in love with someone else, someone more outgoing and much prettier than me."

He let that soak in, mentally deciding he'd ask her about her lost love and her broken heart later, when she was ready to tell him about it. "I'm sorry you had to go through that, but I don't want to be a replacement, Ana. I want you to see me for myself, flaws and all." And he wanted her to love him. Oh, how he wanted that.

"And will you accept me, flaws and all?" she asked, the words holding a hint of hope.

"Absolutely. If I spot a flaw in you, I'll let you know."

He heard her sigh, saw her doubt turn into a gentle smile. "We could have a chance here, Ana. A good chance, with prayer and patience, to find the things that have been missing in our lives."

"You do make it sound like business. Like some sort of contract to be ironed out and negotiated."

"I didn't mean it that way," he said, wondering when he'd started repeating himself. "Look, it just seems as if we're both scared of taking things further, for whatever reasons. I'm only asking you to meet me halfway, to be honest with me. I think you feel the same way. I just wanted you to know…I'm willing to try."

"Even though it might be painful?"

"It's a really nice sort of pain."

"Okay." She walked toward him and grabbed the lapels of his shirt, a soft sigh of release shuddering through her. "I guess it is time for the next step."

Then she kissed him, long and hard, and with

such a sweet intensity that he almost fell back into the wet, churning surf.

But Rock didn't fall. Ana caught him just in time.

She was dreaming of Rock. It was a sweet dream, muted in shades of yellow sunset and pink sky, tinged with a kind of contentment that flowed like cool water over her soul. In the dream, Rock was kissing her beside the ocean. She was wearing the shrunken dress. There was an owl sitting on a tree in the background. Ana felt safe, completely at home.

"Aunt Ana, wake up!"

The voice shrilling in her ear brought Ana out of her dreams. She sat up in bed and stared groggily out into the darkness, her breathing shallow and swift. The clock on the bedside table said four a.m. "Marybeth? What is it, honey?"

Marybeth stood fidgeting at the side of the bed, her big green eyes bright with fear. "It's Laurel. She sneaked out to meet Cal on the beach. She was supposed to be back by now, but...well, it's been hours and hours and she's not home yet. Aunt Ana, I'm so worried."

Chapter Twelve

"Start at the beginning," Ana told Marybeth. They were in the kitchen with Rock, Eloise and Cal's father, Don. It was five o'clock in the morning.

Marybeth sighed, glancing toward where Rock stood making coffee. "It's okay, honey," he said. "We just need to know the truth."

"All I know is that Laurel really, really likes Cal and he likes her, too. They decided to sneak out, to go down to the beach for a midnight stroll or swim or something." She shrugged. "I told her she'd get into trouble. Now she's going to blame me for tattling."

"It's okay to tattle when someone could be in trouble or in danger," Eloise pointed out.

Ana closed her eyes, remembering those first terrifying moments after Marybeth had told her Laurel was missing. Not knowing where else to turn, she'd called Rock first. He knew the island. He might have an idea where Cal would take Laurel. He'd called Eloise. Ana was glad for the older woman's quiet strength.

"Cal knows better," his father, a bulky man with shots of silver in his spiky hair, said as Rock handed him a cup of steaming coffee. "That kid— he sees a pretty girl and all of the sense just leaves his brains."

Rock smiled. "It happens to the best of us," he said, glancing at Ana. "I'm sure they're okay."

"I can't stand waiting," Ana said, slipping off her stool to pace the room. "Why haven't the police called?"

"They're looking out near the lighthouse, Ana," Eloise said. "Although I must say, Chief Anderson didn't seem that concerned. That man's gotten so lackadaisical, he needs to retire." Ana didn't miss the glance that passed between mother and son.

"You think something's happened, don't you," she said, her heart fluttering with fear. "What is it, Rock?"

Rock put down his coffee, then pulled her around. "I'm sure they're okay, but...if they decided to go for a swim...well, those midnight tides can be very dangerous."

"You mean the undertow?"

"Yes, that and the fact that sharks like to troll these waters after dark."

"Sharks?" Ana sank back down against the stool. "I can't believe this is happening. Tara trusted me—" Her hand went to her mouth. "I have to call Tara."

Rock shook his head. "Let's give it some more time. If we haven't found them by daylight, then we'll call her."

Ana grabbed his arm. "Take me out there, Rock, please. Just drive me around the island. I can't stay here. I'll go crazy with worry."

Rock looked at Eloise. She nodded. "I'll stay here with the girls. Don will keep me company, won't you, Don?"

"Yeah, sure," Don said, his gray eyes widening. "Rock, you'll call us if—"

"If I hear or see anything, I promise," Rock said, already guiding Ana toward the door.

Rock had driven his small pickup instead of the big work van. Ana climbed inside, glad for the closeness the tiny vehicle allowed. "I should have seen this coming," she said, her eyes scanning the predawn darkness. "Laurel has been having a hard time dealing with her father's death. Tara told me she's been acting out. At times, she appears completely normal, then other times, she's very rude to her mother and snarly to everyone else."

"That's understandable," Rock said, his eyes on the road that ran along the beach. "I remember how confused I was at that age, especially after losing my father. I guess I've been blaming my mother for a lot of things that weren't really her fault."

"But…you're trying," Ana said, willing the chatter to calm her mind and steady her nerves so she could think. "You and Eloise seems close."

"We are now," Rock said, slowing to scan the picnic tables scattered across a roadside park. "It took many, many years and a lot of prayer, but we're making progress."

"I hope Laurel can find some sort of peace," Ana said. Then she ran a hand over her hair. "I hope they…didn't do anything stupid." She inhaled a long, shuddering breath. "Rock, she's only fourteen. I should have been more aware. I shouldn't have let things distract me—"

"It's going to be all right," Rock said, reaching across the space between them to clasp her hand in his. "And don't go blaming yourself. You've monitored those girls day and night. You have to sleep sometime, and besides, we had no inkling that she'd pull a stunt like this."

"She's so confused and hurt," Ana said, her hand gripping the handle on the truck door as she searched for movement in the trees and on the beaches as they passed. "I just wish I'd taken more time to talk with her. I've had them for two weeks, and now this.''

Rock slowed the truck to search a tiny inlet where the ocean curved into the bay. ''In spite of her hostility, I think Laurel has a good head on her shoulders. And Cal is a good boy. He has four older sisters who've turned out all right, and they lost their mother. Laurel probably thought she wouldn't get caught, or they could have just lost track of time.''

''I hope it's that. I can handle that, but I can't handle something happening to them.''

They fell silent as they searched the dunes and shores on the far west side of the island near the lighthouse, sometimes getting out to walk along the lonely, empty stretches of beach. But they didn't see Laurel and Cal.

An hour later, as the sun began to climb up over the eastern waters, Ana knew she'd waited long enough.

''I have to call Tara.''

Rock nodded. ''We'll make one more sweep. Let's go up Lady Street, just to see if maybe they're at one of the coffee shops. Then, if we don't find them, we'll go home and call her.''

''Thank you,'' Ana said, sincerely meaning it. ''I don't usually fall apart like this, but...she's so young and I feel so responsible.'' She also felt guilty, very guilty. She'd been so wrapped up in her newfound feelings for Rock that she had neglected everything else around her, first her work, and now her nieces. Maybe it was time for her to concentrate on both again.

Rock was watching her as if he could read exactly what she was thinking. "This isn't your fault, you know. Teenagers are wily, Ana. You can't predict their moves. You just have to give them guidance and hope for the best."

"But what if the worst happens?"

Rock stopped the truck in front of the closed amusement park. "I don't know what to tell you. I don't expect the worst, but if it happens, we'll deal with it, together."

"Maybe that's part of the problem," Ana said, at her wits' end. "Maybe we've been together too much, so much that I've failed Laurel. I should have paid closer attention."

"Don't talk like that."

Ana opened the truck door and got out before he could reach for her. Her emotions had reached a fever pitch. Dashing tears away, she scanned the distant shore, her eyes touching on the Wedding Rock out past the Sunken Pier Restaurant. Remembering when Rock had brought her here, she wished she'd remembered her pledge to keep things strictly business between them. If she had, she might have been more in tune to Laurel's problems, and the girl's obvious interest in Cal Ashworth. Ana glanced back out into the muted darkness, her mind racing with the possibility of sharks and undertows.

And that's when she saw them. Laurel and Cal.

Barely visible because of the dark dawn, they were sitting up against one side of the rock, facing away from the water. Cal had his arm around Laurel and it looked as if they were asleep.

"Laurel!" Ana started running toward them, her hands waving in the air as she shouted. "Laurel?"

Her voice carried on the morning wind, echoing out over the buildings and sand. Laurel jerked her head up, saw her aunt coming, then shook Cal out of his sleep. "Aunt Ana?"

Ana cried tears of pure joy. "Laurel, are you all right?" She kept running toward them.

"I'm fine," Laurel called. Cal helped her up, and together, they started toward Ana. Then Laurel raised a hand in warning. "Aunt Ana, look out!"

It was too late for Ana, though. She didn't see the deep hole in the sand. Still running, she hit the hole and slipped, feeling nothing under her left foot. Then she fell and went rolling against the sandy, seashell-covered lane leading down to the shore.

A sharp, distinct pain burned its way up Ana's left foot and leg as one foot sank into the giant water-filled hole and she pitched forward, her face hitting the sand as she let out a tortured scream.

Rock was at her side. "Ana? Are you all right?"

"No," she said, pushing up on her hands, sand in her mouth. Her cheekbone burned from scraping the tiny shells and rocks. "I think I sprained my ankle."

Rock gently lifted her up into a sitting position, dusting off her face and clothes, while Laurel and Cal came hurrying to stand wide-eyed beside her.

"Aunt Ana?" Laurel said, her voice trembling with fear. "I'm so sorry."

Rock held Ana, then turned to the two teenagers. "You two have some explaining to do. But we need to get your Aunt to a doctor first."

"No," Ana said, trying to stand. She grimaced, the pain in her foot unbearable. "I'll be okay. Just get me home."

"You've hurt your foot," Rock said, lifting her into his arms. "I'm taking you by the medical center."

"I think he's right," Cal said, his hand in Laurel's.

Ana looked over Rock's shoulder at her niece. "Just tell me you're okay, Laurel. I've been so worried—"

"I'm fine," Laurel said sheepishly. "We went for a walk and, well, we sat down by the Wedding Rock to talk and—"

"We fell asleep," Cal finished. "We were tired

and we just fell asleep. That's the truth, Ms. Hanson.''

Ana didn't know if her tears were from joy or pain, or both. But she finally gave in to them. ''They were tired. They fell asleep,'' she said through gulps as she looked up at Rock. ''No sharks, no undertows...thank goodness.''

''We'll either hug them or throttle them later,'' Rock said as he kissed her forehead. ''Right now, I'm taking you to a doctor.''

Ana snuggled against him, acutely aware of the strength of his arms, of the warmth of his heart beating against her ear.

This is what got you into this mess, she reminded herself. In a little while, after the pain had ebbed, after the shock of her niece missing all night had worn off, Ana would have to take a step back and evaluate the twists and turns of her mixed-up life.

In a little while. Right now, she couldn't help herself. She wanted to stay safe in Rock's arms.

The next afternoon, Tara paced the floor of Ana's long, sun-dappled second-floor bedroom. ''I can't believe this.''

''Believe it,'' Ana said, wincing as she shifted her heavily bandaged ankle. ''Your daughter spent the night out on the beach with Cal Ashworth, I have a severely sprained ankle, and the tea room is set to open this weekend.''

"What are we going to do?" Tara said. "I'm due back in Savannah tomorrow, for a conference on this Atlanta land deal, and I'm still in negotiation with some mystery man about that land near Savannah—extremely sensitive negotiations."

"I never expected you to help with the opening," Ana said. "I'll manage, somehow." She wanted to shake her sister into seeing that Laurel needed her right now, but decided she'd refrain from that tactic.

"How?" Tara gestured at her ankle. "You can't walk, Ana. How are you going to cook and supervise the opening? Not to mention that we now have to watch Laurel's every move, restriction or not."

Ana wondered that herself. Since yesterday, she'd been stuck here in her bedroom, with her throbbing ankle up on a pillow, encased off and on in ice packs. That meant she hadn't really had much of a chance to talk to Laurel. Then Tara had come home today, in a rage about what Laurel had done. She'd immediately put Laurel on restriction, forbidding her to see or speak to Cal for the rest of the summer. Ana wasn't so sure that was the answer to Laurel's problems, but Tara was in such a tizzy, she wouldn't listen to Ana's pleas for mercy on Laurel's behalf.

"Jackie is capable of overseeing things," Ana said, glad she'd hired an assistant already trained in running a restaurant. "And Tina is a great hostess. Plus, my waiters and waitresses have been training for weeks now.''

"But...this has to be a good opening." Tara stopped, shook her head. "I'm staying here. I'll just explain to my boss that my sister needs me."

"And your daughter," Ana said. Tara glanced down at her, perplexed. "Laurel needs you, too, Tara."

Tara sank down on a white ottoman. "I know she does. Tell me how...how can I reach her? She won't even talk to me anymore." She held her hair back with her hand. "We used to be so close and now...she's changing right before my eyes. I think she honestly hates me."

Ana moved the ice pack off her leg. "She doesn't hate you. She's just still mourning her father. She's confused and her hormones are going berserk. She might not talk to you, but if she sees that you care, that will help."

"So...all the more reason for me to stay here."

"If you do, do it for Laurel, not me," Ana said, trying to shift to a more comfortable position. "But you said yourself this deal was important. You have to decide."

"The Atlanta deal is almost done," Tara said. "I can stall them a couple of days. And as for the land I'm trying to sell—my land—well, Mr. Big Shot, whoever he is, can just stew until he gives me the asking price I want. You're right, Ana, you need me now, and so do my children. I can't leave you with my daughters and a restaurant to run, too—and with a hurt foot.''

"Okay, we'll talk more about this later," Ana replied, the pain medicine Doc Sanders had given her kicking in. "I plan on being better tomorrow, anyway.''

A knock at the door made Tara spin around. "Do you want visitors?''

"It's probably Jackie," Ana said, motioning for Tara to open the door. "We've got some last-minute decisions to make—a few minor concerns.''

Tara threw up her hands, then opened the door. Turning to Ana, she smiled slyly. "It's not Jackie.''

Before Ana could ask who was at her bedroom door, Rock walked in, carrying a tray complete with a daisy and some tea and cookies. He filled the feminine white-and-yellow room with a distinctly male presence. "Jackie said she needed someone to test the white-chocolate cookies and raspberry-peach tea.''

"I've had both," Ana said, wishing she'd had time to comb her hair, at least.

"Well, now you can have both again." He set the white wicker tray across the bed. "I brought extra." Turning to Tara, he offered her a big round cookie.

"No, I don't eat sweets," Tara said, lifting a hand to stop him. "Besides, I've got things to do to get ready for the opening. I'll be downstairs with Jackie if you need me."

Ana watched as her sister beat a hasty exit. "Hyper, that one. Always in a hurry. She has it in her head to stay here and help out. She'll be bossing everyone around."

"Not like you, huh?" Rock's smile was a mixture of appreciation and admiration.

"I'm not moving very fast these days, so I can't really give anyone orders," Ana said, taking time to sip the fragrant tea. "Hmm. Jackie knows how to brew a good strong cup of tea."

"Then, I think your tea room will be a big hit."

"Good. I intend to be there for the opening."

Rock saw the stubborn glint in Ana's eyes. Shaking his head, he said, "Doc Sanders told you to rest for a few days. You're bruised and sore, Ana."

"I've rested. And now I'm ready to get back to work."

"I don't think that's wise."

"Oh, really. Well, I think I don't have any choice. The tea room opens on Saturday and I intend to be downstairs, right in the thick of things. I've worked too hard to miss this."

"But your ankle is sprained. You don't want to do permanent damage."

Ana dropped the cookie she'd been nibbling. "Rock, I have to do this. I can hobble around. I'm used to doing things my way, on my own."

Rock could relate to that. He was the same way himself. He'd had to learn to turn certain matters over to the Lord, though. Or go crazy trying to control them.

"Have you ever thought about letting go of some of that control, of trusting other people, and maybe the good Lord, too, to take care of things for you, just once?"

"Are you calling me a control-freak?"

"No, but you obviously aren't used to letting anyone help you. Maybe this is a sign you should slow down and learn to trust others."

"I do trust," she said. "I trust that my foot will be better tomorrow and I can hobble around and get things going. And I'm praying to God for that to happen."

Rock touched the daisy he'd swiped out of Milly McPherson's yard. "Look, Ana, we're all here to help."

"I appreciate that, but you have your own work."

"I don't mind pitching in."

"You don't like to cook."

"I've cooked all my life. I think I can help out in a tea room."

She laughed out loud, almost choking on her tea.

"What's so funny?"

"The image of you in a pinafore apron, serving tea to little old ladies."

"I'll do it if I must." He leaned closer. "I mean it, Ana. It's part of the new me, the better me. The me that wants to impress Ana Hanson."

He watched as his words settled over her. Ana didn't like being helpless—but then, who did? Deciding to change the subject, he said, "I had a long talk with Laurel this morning."

"Really?"

"Yep. She showed up at my shop. I think she was probably looking for Cal, but she found me, instead."

"That's good. Tara has given her strict orders to stay away from Cal."

"His daddy is handling that end of things, too. He has Cal working on a house way on the other side of the island, pulling up baseboards and tearing out old Sheetrock. Hot, sweaty work and real torture, eight hours a day for the next two weeks."

"Well, at least Don listened when Cal tried to explain. He seems like a reasonable parent."

"He believes in love and discipline. And respect."

"I wish Tara had at least talked to Laurel. She just shouted at her and sent her to her room."

"A mistake many well-meaning parents make every day."

"So what did Laurel say to you?"

He sighed, raked a hand down his chin. "Not much at first. I made small talk, let her hammer a few nails and glue a few dadoes and tenons on a small cabinet I've been working on. She finally opened up."

"What did she say?"

"It's what she didn't say that has me concerned," Rock told her. "Laurel clearly thinks she's somehow responsible for her father's death."

Ana shot up, winced, then sank back against the pillows. "Why would she think that?"

Rock shrugged. "I don't know. She did tell me that her parents had been fighting a lot before Chad died. She said they weren't really happy. Then she said something very odd."

"What?"

Rock debated telling Ana this, but decided she had to know. And he needed some answers himself. "She said her father never really loved her mother. That he'd been in love with another woman before he met her mother. Laurel seems to think he still had feelings for that other woman."

Ana's hand went to her mouth, her face flushing hot. "Oh, my goodness. I wonder what would make her think such a thing?"

Rock leaned close, his hands on either side of Ana's lacy pillows. "I wonder that, too, Ana. And

I'm really wondering who this other woman was. In fact, I've been wondering a lot of things regarding you and your sister. Care to explain any of this to me?''

Chapter Thirteen

"I don't know what you mean," Ana said, her heart thumping so loud that she was sure Rock could hear it.

"I remember you saying you were dumped in college. You said he fell in love with another woman."

"That's true."

"Well, I also remember you saying your sister was the pretty, outgoing one, and that this man fell for a woman who was pretty and more outgoing than you."

"That's very true."

"You've dropped enough hints, Ana. I think I have it figured out. Did your college sweetheart leave you for your sister?"

Ana lowered her gaze and stared down into her tea as if it could give her answers. "Yes," she said finally. "Chad and I had been together for almost two years. I'd never brought him home to meet my family." She stopped, set her teacup down. "Then Tara decided to attend college in Savannah, with me. Naturally, I wanted to protect her, help her around campus. Chad was more than happy to help out, too. Before the fall semester was over, he was in love with Tara. But they didn't bother telling me that until much later."

Rock lifted her chin with a finger, his eyes full of compassion and understanding. "That must have been rough on you, knowing how they felt."

"I couldn't be sure," she said, her voice shuddering. "We all kind of tap-danced around it for months. Then Chad came to me and told me we needed to break up. I didn't even question him. I just let him go."

"You didn't try to fight it?"

"No, why should I? Tara was…is so beautiful. All that blond hair and those big blue eyes. We are so very different."

He stared at her for such a long time, the heat of it sent a blush up her face. But he didn't try to argue with her. "So you thought—"

"I thought I was doing what was best for all of us. I let him go because I could tell he was in love with Tara."

Rock dropped his hand away from her face, then settled back on the side of the bed. "Did you ever question things? Did you ever talk to Tara and Chad about this?"

"No. Tara finally came to me after Chad and I broke up. She poured out her heart to me, cried with me. I forgave her, because I love her. I knew I could never be happy with Chad, knowing he'd rather be with my sister. And I couldn't find it in my heart to hate her."

"But you never talked to Chad about this?"

"No. Things were awkward after that. I tried to avoid him. The next time I saw him up close and personal was at their wedding that spring." She shifted on her pillows. "Look, it was a long time ago. We all got along fine, once things settled down. Chad and Tara had Laurel soon after they were married, and I was overjoyed to be an aunt, so I put all of that aside."

"Then, why does Laurel think her father didn't love her mother?"

"I don't know. Maybe because when she heard them fighting, it looked or sounded that way. But they loved each other. I know they did."

He leaned forward, the intensity of his gaze washing Ana in a soft, heated light. "You are a remarkable woman, Ana. You forgave your sister for taking away the man you loved. You've been a loving aunt to her children."

"She didn't take him away. I never had him."

"I wouldn't be so sure about that," Rock said, his hand moving up her arm.

"What do you mean?"

"Nothing. Never mind. Let's just concentrate on getting you well, and getting Laurel through this rough spot."

Ana grabbed his hand, stopping him from getting any closer. "Rock, you don't think—I mean there is no way Chad still had feelings for me even after all that time. He loved me once, but not after Tara. Once they were together, he only had eyes for her."

"I don't know. I only know that Laurel heard something to trigger all of these doubts and fears. But I think there is a possibility that, yes, Chad still loved you. Maybe he loved both of you, but in different ways."

Ana had certainly believed Chad loved her once. But that was before Tara…or was it? "Is that possible?"

"Anything is possible," he replied. "But I need to know how *you* felt about Chad—how you still feel about Chad."

Ana swallowed, saw the raw need in his eyes. "Oh, Rock, I'm so sorry. All this time, you must have been thinking I've been pining away for a man I could never have."

"Have you? Are you still carrying a torch for Chad Parnell?"

Ana leaned forward, her hands clasping the front of his shirt. "No," she said, her whispered word full of longing and hope. "I accepted that he loved Tara. I'd be lying if I said I didn't think about him now and again, and I did harbor a good dose of bitterness. But I kept that bitterness to myself, to avoid hurting my family, especially my parents. They don't know any of this, and I refuse to feud with my only sister. Besides, my sister and her daughters are as close to a family—children, I mean—as I've come. I did make some bad decisions in the relationship department, I think maybe because I thought I'd lost my one chance when I lost Chad. But I stopped loving him in that way a very long time ago. We were civil to each other, friends for the sake of our family. But…I'm okay, really."

"Really?"

"Yes," she said as she put a hand on his face. "Lately, I've held out hope for another man."

His smile was soft, and filled with immediate relief. "Do I know this other man?"

"I think you do. He's a paradox, though. Always changing right before my eyes. He surprises me every day."

He scowled. "Who is this mysterious man?"

"Don't tell," she said as she leaned close and

whispered in his ear. "He's a very good carpenter and he also happens to be a minister. What more could a girl ask?"

With that, she kissed him, her mouth fluttering across his face before settling on his waiting lips.

Rock sank against her, holding her, kissing her back with a gentle force that took Ana's balance completely away.

Then he released her and looked down at her. "He's one lucky man, I think."

Ana stared up at him, thinking she just might be the lucky one, the blessed one, at last. The image of that kind of intense happiness made it hard for her to find her next breath. Her fear ran deep.

"We have to take things slow," she told him, her voice ragged. "I don't want to make another mistake."

"I understand. Besides, we have a tea room to operate."

"We?" The surprise in her voice surely showed in her eyes. "This coming from a man who only wants an old-fashioned stay-at-home kind of woman?"

"I never said that. I'll admit I had these silly notions, but as you said, I'm changing all the time."

"So you're willing to…cook and wear an apron to help me serve my customers?"

"I told you I'd do it for you. And I told you

when we first met, we all pitch in around here, Ana. We help each other, even if it means... wearing an apron. I intend to help you, whether you like it or not.''

She was thinking she liked it. More than a lot. Ana sat in a comfortable wicker chair in a corner of the kitchen, pillows all around her, her bandaged foot elevated on a matching footstool, while she watched her dream taking shape. An added bonus, Greta Epperson was doing an exclusive story on the tea room, minus the gossip and innuendo.

''So,'' Greta said now, her pen in her red-lipped mouth, her big black-framed glasses sitting on top of her tuft of white hair, ''where were we? Oh, yes. You met Eloise in Savannah and she persuaded you to consider opening the tea room here on Sunset Island?''

''Yes,'' Ana said, repeating the story of her goal to run her own business. As she talked to Greta, she smiled and sighed. Her goal, her dream was about to happen.

With the help of almost everyone she knew.

Cal and his father were busy stocking the pantry and making sure all the new cabinets were in working order, even though they'd been checked and rechecked. Cal worked silently and steadily, but Ana saw him glance at Laurel each time she passed by. The boy had it bad, apparently. And he was suffering.

Ana was reminded of how Rock was willing to suffer for her. While she didn't want either of them to suffer, Ana had to admit it was nice to know that some men would go to great lengths for their women. But was she truly Rock's woman? Contrary to what the whole island thought, she still had to wonder.

And contrary to what Laurel hoped and dreamed for, Ana knew it could all change in a heartbeat. But right now, hurt feelings and confused hearts would have to be put aside. Ana's Tea Room and Art Gallery was opening the day after tomorrow.

Eloise had formed the girls into a team. They were coming and going, setting tables and polishing glasses, placing napkins in napkin rings and making sure the menus were in their protective covers and ready to hand out on Saturday. Laurel had been especially nice and cooperative, since she obviously felt responsible for Ana's having hurt her foot.

Jackie was issuing orders to the waitstaff. ''You, put that stack of napkins in the buffet drawer. Hey, you over there—Charlotte—make sure those teapot caddies are ready. And would someone please check the table arrangements one more time and make sure everyone has been assigned enough tables to wait?''

Tina ran around mostly being nervous, the stress
on her face obvious as she bullied everyone into
practicing being customers. "C'mon," she said,
her short brown hair standing on end as she herded
all the workers toward tables. "Act like you're
starving and need a strong cup of tea. We'll give
you free samples of lunch for your trouble."

She immediately got several hungry volunteers,
especially when Milly McPherson showed up, intent on making sure that Ana's first batch of Brunswick stew, which they'd all worked on together
last night, had Milly's personal stamp of approval.

"If it's going to be called Miss Milly's Brunswick Stew, then it's going to have Milly's hand in
it," the old woman had stubbornly told them. In
the end, all the women and the three girls, too, had
a hand in Milly's stew. They'd cooked, chopped,
stirred, tasted and laughed and talked about everything from flowers to men.

Sitting here now, Ana remembered last night's
conversation.

"I think a wedding's coming," Milly had announced, her keen eyes on Ana as she sat with her
foot propped high.

"You think so, Milly?" Eloise asked as she
dumped English peas in with the pork, beef and
chicken that had been slow-cooked all day in prep-
aration for the stew.

"Preacher Rock has that lovesick look about

him," Milly replied, nodding her approval at both the carrots Tara had sliced and the preacher's choice for a bride. "'Course, he's more of a carpenter than a preacher," Milly added, snickering. "God love him, he never did know how to preach a fire-and-brimstone sermon—all that philosophy and quoting poetry goes right over the head of some of us. But he's passable enough to get us into heaven, I reckon. And he's got a good steady income from his carpentry work."

"There's a certain spirituality in being a carpenter," Eloise pointed out. "Jesus was a carpenter." She stirred the stew, then grabbed a cookie. "Rock is an artist, and he does have a way with words at times. Either way, there is no shame in being a carpenter's wife, Ana."

"The carpenter's wife," Marybeth teased.

Soon, the echo had sounded throughout the kitchen as Tara and the other girls, along with Jackie and Tina, and even the timid new waitress, Charlotte, took up the chant.

The carpenter's wife.

Ana let that soak in as she now watched her family and friends put together the plans she'd held to her heart for so long.

Did she want to be the carpenter's wife? Did she want to be a preacher's wife? It would be so easy to slip into the slow, steady life here on the island. Sundays in church with Rock, Sunday dinner out on the beach, or maybe inside on a picnic blanket on a rainy afternoon. And then later—Ana stopped her thoughts right there. Rock might not be ready for a wife. Maybe he just liked having a friend, even if he had asked her to take things to the next level. A friend that he kissed now and again—more now than again, she reminded herself.

Deciding to concentrate on the here and now, rather than what might be, Ana smiled as her sister whizzed by in a huff of expensive perfume. "Slow down," she teased, laughing as Tara called out instructions to Don and Cal.

"Watch that light fixture, guys!"

Tara was in charge of making sure all the artwork and knickknacks were being displayed, paying special attention to a piece Eloise had created to celebrate the opening. It was a cutout of a little girl, her Victorian-style hooped dress and big rounded hat formed and joined by welded pieces of iron.

There were other works by Eloise, plus several beautiful watercolors and seascapes by various island artists. These were showcased among vintage hats and purses, miniature ceramic shoes, antique and art deco jewelry and a host of other items such as dishes, soaps and perfumes, candles, and dainty quilted satin walking jackets designed and hand-painted by yet another local.

"It's coming together nicely, dear," Eloise said

as she brought Ana another cup of green tea. "Drink this—loaded with antioxidants."

"Will it make me walk again?" Ana asked, her sarcasm making Eloise frown. "Sorry. I just hate sitting here, doing nothing."

"You're supervising," Rock said from around the corner. He was in charge of the final kitchen details, which included everything from checking the industrial-size stove to making sure the refrigerator and walk-in freezer were stocked with the needed items for tomorrow's lunch and open house. "And may I add, you look absolutely beautiful, just sitting there." He winked, then disappeared before Ana could dispute his words.

"He's in love with you," Eloise said, clasping her hands together as if in prayer.

"What makes you think that?" Ana asked, as a warm surge of longing pierced her heart.

"Why, the way he looks at you, the way he's going beyond the call of duty to help you with this," Eloise explained. "You must have figured by now—Rock wants a traditional wife. He's always balked at career women. Too much like dear old mom. And he especially avoids anyone connected with any form of the arts—too whimsical and flighty—just like dear old mom."

"I do understand that about him," Ana said, amazed that Eloise knew her son so very well.

"So…how can he be in love with me, since I'm involved in a career *and* I love art?"

Eloise sank down on the wide, cushioned footstool, careful not to bother Ana's wrapped ankle. "That's the pure beauty of it. He's fought against those things all of his life, but low and behold, you come along and…he's had to stop fighting. It's no longer an issue—what you do or don't do, whether you're a traditional kind of woman or not. You've got qualities he admires, and you've also got qualities that frighten him. Rock loves you in spite of his greatest fears. That's true love, darling."

Ana swallowed and closed her eyes, afraid to hope. "Is that how you felt about Rock's father?"

"Absolutely," Eloise replied. "I loved Tillman Dempsey from the moment I set eyes on him walking along the beach. And in spite of everything I had to endure, loving him and having him for the time I did was worth all of it."

"But you gave up so much."

"I gave up nothing. Material things only. I gained a true treasure, Ana. I had love, so much love."

Ana saw the tears well in Eloise's gray eyes. "How did you cope…after he died?"

"Not very well," Eloise said, her voice going soft. "I didn't always do things right. I had to learn the hard way. I became a success in my work, but I was a miserable failure with my sons."

"But Rock loves you."

"Yes, because Rock is noble and good and respectful. He has all the qualities that are admirable in a man."

"Do you think he loves you out of duty?"

"No," Eloise said, getting up to return to work. "Rock loves with his heart. And I know he loves you. It just might take a while for him to figure that out."

"I'm still not sure…about us," Ana said. "I don't know if Rock can handle this." She gestured to indicate the tea room. "And I can't let go. I need this."

"You don't have to give up your dream," Eloise told her. "You're much wiser than I was. You can have it all, Ana. You know how to balance love and work. I didn't."

Ana wondered if Eloise could see how scared she was. She wasn't sure she could balance anything. For so long, she'd dreamed of owning her own business. On the other hand, in her secret heart, she'd also longed for a family. A traditional family where she raised children and took care of a home and husband.

Suddenly, she could see that she and Rock weren't so very different, after all.

Eloise watched her, as if sensing her turmoil and her realizations. "It takes compromise, Ana. I never learned that. I was too wrapped in grief and ambition to see the treasures God had given me. When I think of all the times I shooed my children away so I could work one more hour, one more late night, I wish now I could turn back time and stop everything, just to see their young faces again. Those faces were so full of hope and questions, so full of need and grief. I failed my sons when they were growing up, at a time when they needed me most. I've promised God I will make it up to them now. That's why I'm pushing them so hard to find families of their own. I robbed them of that. With God's help, I aim to give back what I took away.''

Eloise got up, and turned to find Rock standing there looking at her. Ana saw by the expression on his face that what he had overheard had been a revelation. He'd obviously overheard Eloise.

''Mother?'' he said, his eyes misty, his voice low and gravelly.

Eloise's hand went to her throat, but she didn't speak.

Rock hurried to her, touched her face. ''Mother, you owe me nothing, do you understand? I was wrong to make you think so.''

''Yes, I do,'' Eloise said, bobbing her head. ''So much. I can never make up for all that lost time, but…I can pray that you find happiness. And that you finally forgive me.''

Unable to speak, Rock pulled his mother into

his arms. "I think I'm the one who needs forgiving."

Ana felt tears piercing her eyes. She'd never seen Rock show his mother this type of affection. He'd touch her face, smile at her conversation, but he'd never once reached beyond the wall he'd built around himself. Today, here in her kitchen, in the midst of all the commotion and chaos, Rock was holding his mother to his heart.

Ana bit back her own tears and quelled her worries. She knew she'd just witnessed one of God's tender mercies—the forgiveness of a son for a mother, the love of a mother for a son, the unconditional understanding that only a strong faith could bring. A light shone down on Eloise and Rock, maybe the sun streaming through the wide, shining-clean windows, maybe a ray of hope from heaven itself. But the light was there, washing them in redemption and joy.

Ana closed her eyes, let the light wash over her, too, and knew that God had brought her to this place.

When she opened her eyes, Rock was looking down at her, his expression full of tenderness and understanding.

"We've got a lot of work left to do," he said, releasing his mother with a shaky smile.

Ana got the impression he wasn't talking about just her tea room.

Chapter Fourteen

❧

"You don't have to look so blue," Tara told Ana the morning of the tea room's opening. "Everything is in place and we're ready to go."

Ana tried to muster up a smile, but all she really wanted to do was sit down and have a good cry. She didn't understand why she felt this way. Maybe the opening was just anticlimactic after all the hustle and bustle of *getting there*. Or maybe she was just too confused about her feelings for Rock. She still remembered his words from yesterday. *"We've got a lot of work left to do."*

The way he'd looked at her, the way he'd hugged his mother, told her that Rock was going through the same doubts and fears that she was having. Love shouldn't be this complicated.

"Is it your ankle?" Tara asked, concern marring her expression. "Does it hurt?"

"My ankle is much better," Ana said, wishing this ache were from a physical pain.

Tara brushed at the bedspread. "Then, you're going to have to clue me in, sis. We can't have you looking like that with guests coming for lunch."

"I know, I know," Ana said, hobbling over to her jewelry box to find her pearl earrings. "I...can't explain it. I finally have everything I've dreamed about for so long, but—"

"But it's not enough?" Tara asked, coming to stand by her. Their eyes met in the mirror.

"Yes," Ana said, nodding. "How did you know?"

Tara shook her head, then turned Ana around. "I felt that way after I became successful in real estate. I worked so hard, stayed late almost every day, won sales awards, but one day I looked out the window of my office and noticed an ancient oak tree for the first time. I'd never even seen that tree before, hadn't even realized it was there. On this particular spring morning, that old oak was so beautiful it took my breath away. I got to wondering what else I was missing."

Ana sank on the bed, careful not to wrinkle her white linen sheath. "Did you feel as if something was wrong? As if you were having all these doubts and fears and you just wanted to run in the other direction?"

"I sure did," Tara replied, her blue eyes deepening with memories. "Chad and I...things were shaky in the years before he died. I sat there, remembering the fight we'd had the night before, and I wondered about that tree. What had that beautiful tree witnessed? What had it seen and heard? How had God protected it through the centuries? I asked myself, was God protecting me like that?"

"Did you want that—God's protection?"

"Oh, yes. I just wasn't sure how to find it. I'm still searching."

"I guess we all are," Ana said. Then she did smile. "Rock has helped me so much with that."

"Well, he is a preacher."

"Does that bother you?"

"Why should it?" Tara asked. "I can use some spiritual guidance, that's for sure. And Rock is a good, kind man. He doesn't pass judgment. He just listens. He's helped me with Laurel, with trying to understand her and not reprimand her so much. Until I sat down with Rock, I never realized that I don't actually talk to Laurel. I mostly just nag her. Rock made me see I'd get a whole lot more accomplished with my daughter if I just tried listening to her and talking to her."

"I'm glad he's helped you," Ana said, wishing

she could find the courage to sit and pour out her heart to Rock.

"So what's the problem?" Tara asked, her arms crossed over her red knit dress. "I mean, Rock seems like the sort of man any woman would love to be involved with." Then she held up a hand. "Myself excluded, of course. I don't intend to go down that path again." Making a face, she added, "Besides, that man only has eyes for you."

Ana looked down at the planked floor. "I don't know what to do about him."

Tara laughed, then sat beside Ana. "Why don't you just enjoy being with him?"

"I've tried that. But…we seem to make each other miserable." Ana tucked a pillow up against the headboard. "I mean, we have fun together, we laugh, we talk. He quotes poems and philosophy and Bible verses to me. But it's as if we're dancing around the real issue."

"Which is?"

"Which is…I'm afraid I'll have to give up my identity, myself, in order to be the kind of woman Rock expects me to be."

"Has he tried to change you?" Tara asked, the protective ire in her eyes making Ana smile.

"No. That's just it. After that first horrible fight we had, he's been a perfect gentleman. He said he was willing to suffer to be with me. And that's part of the problem, I think."

Tara frowned, then touched a hand to Ana's arm. "You're not making sense."

Ana let out a sigh, then shrugged. "Rock is doing all the changing. He's willing to change for me. I'm not so sure I can allow him to do that. I don't know if I can accept that."

Tara got up, her charm bracelets dangling. "A man is willing to change for you, and you can't accept that? Ana, is there something seriously wrong with you, girl?"

"There must be," Ana said, getting up to hobble over to the armoire against which her crutches were leaning. "Maybe I expect too much. Maybe I never thought I'd find someone who'd be willing to do that."

"Is this about Chad?" Tara asked out of the blue, her hands going to her hips.

"Chad?" Ana felt the shock of his name all the way to her toes. "What does this have to do with Chad?"

"You loved him once, Ana. Before I came along and ruined things for both of you."

"Ruined things? You married him. You have three beautiful daughters. You had a life."

"Yes, I had the life *you* always wanted. Maybe this tea room has been just a substitute for all that you think you missed. Maybe that's why you're feeling so let-down now. Because, in spite of your dream, you still aren't truly happy."

Ana looked away from Tara's direct gaze. She didn't want her sister to see the truth in her eyes. This dream had been a way of coming close to all the things she longed to have. But she couldn't admit that now. "That's crazy. I have everything I've ever wanted."

"But you're so afraid of accepting Rock's love, you're sitting here in tears."

"I don't want to make a mistake," Ana said, her voice rising with each word. "And I especially don't want Rock to make a mistake. Besides, I don't even know how he really feels. Maybe I'm imagining things."

"You are not imagining." Tara shook her head. "The mistake would be to turn Rock away just because you think you have to be noble and brave, the way you were when you found out about Chad and me. Don't do that, Ana."

All of the anger Ana had held in check for so long came pouring through her. "I wasn't noble and I certainly wasn't brave. I didn't have any choice, Tara. If I recall correctly, Chad dumped me for you. End of discussion."

Tara dropped her arms to her side. "But there never was any discussion. That's just it. You held your feelings so close, Ana, so close. And I've wondered…so many times, what you were truly thinking."

"I was thinking that I had to make a life for

myself, which I've done," Ana said, her heart pierced by the pain she'd tried to hide for so long. "I was trying to…let go. You and Chad were so in love—"

"We shouldn't have gotten married," Tara blurted out. "Do you understand me, Ana? *We*…were the mistake."

"What?" Ana felt the floor shifting underneath her. She had to grab for the brass handle of the armoire to steady herself. "What are you saying?"

Tara wiped tears away, then held up her head. "It wasn't so much love. It was more…lust. What you had with Chad was real love. What I had, well, it was love of a different sort. It was powerful and I was swept away by it. I thought he was my knight in shining armor. Then reality set in. He married me, Ana. But he never forgot you. I think he loved you until the day he died."

Ana's hands groped in the air until she found the nearest chair. "But you seemed so happy—at your wedding and afterwards, all the times I saw you together."

"*Seemed*," Tara repeated, sinking down in front of Ana, her hand reaching for her sister's. "We seemed happy enough and we were at first. We were so caught up in the *notion* of being married, we truly believed everything would work out all right. But things were bad from the beginning. Then right away, I found out I was going to have a baby. Laurel came along and...I loved her with every ounce of my being. I thought surely all the nagging doubts and the little fights would disappear. But Chad—he was indifferent about having a baby. He treated Laurel the same way he treated me, like we were dolls. He showed us off, then expected us to sit on a shelf and behave.''

Ana felt sick to her stomach. ''What about Marybeth and Amanda?''

Tara sighed, sniffed back tears. ''Marybeth was an accident. Chad was furious with me. He didn't want any more children, at least not so soon after Laurel. But he handled it with grace. He had to put up a good front for the world. After all, being a family man got him a big promotion at work. For a while, things got better. We actually planned for another baby, because Chad wanted a boy. Then Amanda came along. He was disappointed, but he hid it right along with everything else he'd managed to hide over the years.''

''I can't believe this,'' Ana said, glancing at the clock. She needed to get downstairs, but she couldn't seem to move. ''All these years—''

''All these years, we were living a lie,'' Tara said, shame in her expression. ''We simply existed for the sake of our children. Chad did love his daughters, in spite of his initial indifference to being a father. I'm thankful for that, at least. But the worst part, the hardest part? Laurel heard us arguing about it—about our sham of a marriage. I don't know exactly what she heard, because a couple of days later, her father was dead and I never got a chance to talk to her about it. And now, she won't talk to me at all. She's closed herself off. She's repeating the same pattern. She's pretending everything is fine, when inside she's hurting. And I think she blames me for the whole thing.''

Ana's heart went out to Tara. Her sister looked so miserable, so full of self-disgust. ''Do you think she knows…everything? That you and Chad didn't love each other? But surely you felt something for each other?''

''We did, but we kept hurting each other. We tried so hard to make it work,'' Tara said, tears in her eyes. ''We tried to find a way back to really loving each other, or at least a way back to how we felt when we first married, but it just got worse. Especially right before he died.''

''And you honestly think Laurel blames you?''

''And herself,'' Tara said. ''I wish she would just talk to me.''

Ana didn't tell Tara what Rock had said. His conversation with Laurel was privileged. Ana wouldn't break the trust that Laurel had found in Rock. That would only make matters worse. ''Have you tried asking her what she heard?''

Tara shook her head. ''I can't seem to find the courage.''

Ana's initial shock had worn down to a numbing hum of confusion. She had to go downstairs and smile and greet her customers, but how, oh how, was she supposed to find the strength to keep this to herself?

"Dear God," she said out loud, her hand clasping Tara's, "we could sure use your guidance right about now."

Tara swallowed back another tear. "My daughter needs you, Lord. I need you, too." Then she smiled over at Ana. "I haven't prayed in a long time. It feels strange, as if I don't deserve it."

"Rock would tell us we both deserve it, simply because God allows us to have second chances," Ana said, rising from the chair. "I'm glad you told me the truth, Tara. Finally."

Tara nodded. "It does feel as if a great weight is off my shoulders. Maybe confession *is* good for the soul."

Ana wiped her eyes, then grinned. "If that's true, then I'm going to feel really good tonight when I open my heart to Rock."

Tara touched her arm. "You're going to tell him you love him?"

Ana nodded, her own anger and grief subdued by what Tara had told her. "I've been nursing this wound about Chad and you for so long, and if I'd only talked to you instead of trying to do what I thought was right...I could have at least helped

you, maybe made Chad see that I held no resentment. I loved him once, but that was long ago. I
can see that so clearly now. I don't know if talking
about it would have made Chad love you any
more, but I just wish you could have shared all this
pain with me before now.'' Getting up, she
brushed at her dress. ''I think I need to quit keeping my feelings tucked inside. Don't you think it's
about time I tell Rock how I really feel, and take
my chances?''

''Long past,'' her sister said. ''And you're right
about Chad and me. We never truly talked things
out, including telling you the truth. We just fussed
and fought. That can't have been good for the girls.
And I know it put a strain on my relationship with
you. I'm sorry for that, Ana.''

''No need to apologize to me,'' Ana replied.
''Chad is gone now. I think in his way, Chad loved
both of us. He tried to make it work with you, and
that's something we can always remember about
him.'' She stopped, looked into Tara's beautiful
eyes. ''All this time, I believed he loved you—the
pretty one, the smart one.''

''When he really loved you just as much,'' Tara
finished. ''I don't feel so very smart or pretty right
now. But that's going to change. I'm going to focus on finding my way back to my children.''

''Now, that is a smart move.''

Tara laughed, swiped at the tear streaks on her face.

"Ana, you're smart and attractive and very worthy of enjoying Rock's love. Please remember that."

"I intend to," Ana said, smiling.

Arms linked, they walked downstairs. Ana grabbed her crutches, but doubted she needed them now. She had her sister and her newfound strength and trust in God to help her find her way.

Tonight, she would tell Rock that she loved him.

He had planned on telling her tonight.

But as Rock watched Ana mingling with the packed-to-capacity luncheon crowd, he knew he'd have to change his plans for them.

He loved her. He saw that now with a clarity as shimmering and crystal clear as the tall, elegant goblets she used to serve her lemon-mint iced tea. He saw that love in the reflection of the cabinets he'd rebuilt and created for her efficient, smooth-running kitchen. Felt that love with each home-cooked dish she urged the pinafore-dressed waitresses to take out to the eager people seated at the bistro tables and the antique lace-covered dining tables where she'd placed them for their first meal at Ana's Tea Room and Art Gallery.

Rock stood back in a quiet corner of the long, busy kitchen, watching Ana's face light up each time a waitress told her how much her table was enjoying the imported hot cinnamon-and-apple tea and blueberry scones, each time Tara rushed in exclaiming she'd just sold yet another work of art, each time Tina and Jackie whispered that the islanders were going crazy over having a place both to buy local art to and eat good food.

He stood out of the way, watching her chat with clients, watching her smile at his mother, who'd been working the crowd like the star she had become, watched as Ana fell right into step in spite of her noticeable limp, saw the way the customers gave her sympathetic pats on the arm, telling her how much they admired her working despite a hurt ankle.

Rock saw that Ana Hanson was a big success.

And as he saw that, he saw their future together slipping right down the drain with the scant leftovers being tossed from the antique china plates. Each *clink* of a glass being filled with ice, each *thump* of a plate being decorated with almond chicken salad or the fruit-and-cheese sampler, only added to Rock's woes. Each cut of the luscious key-lime cheesecake or the decadent dark-chocolate layer cake only reinforced what Rock had felt in his gut since the first day he'd met Ana Hanson.

This woman lived for her work. And it showed in every detail of her rousing debut here today.

Rock couldn't, wouldn't, pull Ana away from that. He couldn't, wouldn't, get involved with her right when she made her dream come true. He didn't expect her to give this up for him and he wouldn't allow her to think he'd want her to do so.

Even though he had.

But had he really expected her to just walk away from this to become a carpenter's wife? A minister's wife?

And good grief, when had he started thinking of her in terms of even *being* his wife?

Probably from the minute he'd laid eyes on her.

Turning away from the hustle and bustle of the kitchen, Rock stepped out onto the long, wrap-around back porch. From this vantage point, he could see the bay to the west. He could hear the seagulls cawing overhead. The sun shone down on the bay, where a slow-trailing sailboat gleamed. The huge, moss-covered oak trees mingled with the ever-waving, tall, elegant palms down toward the shore.

"Why on earth are you standing out here on the porch?" Milly McPherson asked him from the steps, causing Rock to start, his heart hammering.

"Milly? You scared the daylights out of me."

The old woman adjusted the battered, floppy straw hat on her head. "Good. You were way too far into the darkness, from that brooding look on your face.''

''I was just thinking.''

''About this, I 'magine.'' Slowly, she climbed the steps and, with a stern look on her face, handed him a white tissue-wrapped package.

''What is it?'' Rock asked, taking the package Milly unceremoniously shoved at his stomach.

''It's the dress,'' she said, clearly offended by his lack of manners and memory. ''You know, to replace the one you ruined. Ana's dress.''

Ana's dress.

Rock held the soft package as if it were a life line. ''I had forgotten.''

''Well, I didn't. Wanted to finish it in time for her to wear it today, for the opening. But these old fingers and hands didn't want to cooperate. Arthritis ain't pretty.''

Rock took one of Milly's gnarled hands in his. ''These hands are very special. Milly, thank you so much for making the dress. I know Ana will be pleased.'' Then he kissed Milly's hand.

And was rewarded with a gasping, speechless Milly McPherson.

''Well, that's a first,'' he said, grinning.

''Let go of my hand, young man,'' Milly said, quickly hiding her pleased expression behind a tip-lipped nod. Then she batted what was left of her thin eyelashes. "It was my pleasure and a privilege to make a dress for Ana. She is a sweetheart."

She said this last with a meaningful glare at him, as in "And if you mess with her, you have me to contend with."

"That she certainly is," Rock agreed. Then he looked away again, out to the water, seeking answers.

"Are you gonna do right by her?"

Rock looked back at Milly, understanding she came from another generation, wishing he could explain. "I don't know what to do...about Ana."

Milly pushed at her hat. "Don't be daft, boy. You know what needs to be done. Why are you stalling?"

Rock knew he could trust his old friend. "Milly, Ana is happy here, doing what she's always wanted. I don't think I need to interfere with that."

"You *are* off your rocker," Milly huffed. "What makes you think Ana can't handle both you and this business? What makes men think they have to be the be-all-and-end-all for women, anyway?" Before he could defend that statement, she raised a hand. "And don't you dare tell me that you want her to stay at home and cook meals and clean house for you and only you. That would be just too stupid for words."

Feeling duly chastised, Rock cleared his throat. "Well, I *have* always wanted a traditional marriage, and so far, not a woman on this island nor even on the mainland coast of Georgia has wanted to have a second date with me because of that. Now I find Ana—she's beautiful, talented, a very good cook, and surprisingly, she *is* interested in me. We've had much more than a mere date. But she has a life already.''

''And you don't think that life can include you?''

''No, I don't want to make her choose.''

''What makes you think she will have to choose? Women today balance things, same as women have been doing for centuries. I did it. I balanced teaching with helping to raise my nieces and nephews and with counseling and advising most of the children on this island, including you. And contrary to what you think, your own mama tried to balance things.''

Rock bristled at that. ''But…you never married.''

''And your mama never remarried. Ever wonder why?''

No, he hadn't. And he didn't want to delve into that right now. ''I thought we were talking about you, Milly. Meaning no disrespect, but because you never married, how can you understand?''

Milly slapped at his shirtsleeve. ''I *understand* that was *my* choice. Sometimes, I regret that decision. But I still had to balance things out, in my mind. And with the good Lord's guidance, of course. We all do.''

''Of course,'' Rock said, nodding. Milly had certainly opened his eyes to why his mother had locked herself away from the world. Did she only have enough love left for him and his brothers? Maybe she was afraid to love them too much, the way he felt about Ana right now. The way Milly had felt when she'd decided to forget about marriage and a family. Had his mother finally opened her heart to them, before it was too late?

''What if I mess this up?'' he asked Milly. ''What if it's already too late?''

Milly squinted up at him, her small frame seeming awfully formidable. ''Don't miss out on love, son. Go after that woman in there. Anyone with eyes can see that you two are sure-enough in love. I'd hate to see that get lost in the mix of trying to decide who's interfering with whose career. Ana wants to work. She wants to make a life for herself, but—and here's the part where you come in—she also wants exactly what you want—a traditional, loving marriage. Within reason, of course. That's a rare thing these days. Nothing says you can't be a part of that life. You just need to trust in God's plan for you.''

''But, Milly, I've asked God to show me the way, many, many times. I just can't seem to find the answers to this dilemma.''

Milly snorted, her tiny hand on her hip. "Maybe because there is no dilemma, except in your mixed-up head."

"I don't think—"

"Roderick Paul Dempsey, *don't* think, for once. Don't try to philosophize your way out of this one. Just look at what you're holding in your hand."

With that, Milly swept past him into the kitchen, then began issuing stern instructions, to anyone who happened to be passing by, on how to heat up her Brunswick stew without scorching it.

Stunned, Rock looked down at the bundle he held clutched to his stomach. Ana's dress.

Not sure what Milly had meant, he turned and stalked down the steps, headed back to the sanctuary of his little chapel and his workshop. He needed time to think, time to pray. Time to ponder what he should do next. And he needed time to hold Ana's dress close and imagine her wearing it. It might be his last fantasy about Ana Hanson.

Because in his heart, he knew that tonight he would have to tell her that they didn't have a future together. So she could have the future she'd always dreamed about.

At last.

Chapter Fifteen

At last, she could sit down and rest.

Ana smiled at the now-dark kitchen and restaurant area of the house. It was quiet now, settled, still. Like her heart.

The opening had been wonderful. The customers had promised to return and bring friends. And she was already getting calls for private parties. A wedding shower in two weeks. A birthday party next Wednesday at lunch. An anniversary party a month from now—their fiftieth—a surprise from their three children and seven grandchildren.

Ana limped out onto the front porch. A white wicker rocking chair beckoned her. Sinking into the soft flora cushions, she listened to the sound of the ocean. The moonlight cast shimmering silver shadows across the grass and sand, while the wind sang a melancholy song across the sea oats and hibiscus flowers.

She was so tired. But it was a good tired. She wanted to see Rock now. She'd called his cottage and left a message. *"Come by tonight after we close. We'll have leftovers out on the porch."*

So far, Rock hadn't come to see her.

Her heart pounding, Ana decided to take a walk along the sand. Her ankle was still sore, but if she went slowly and was careful, she could make it to the lapping waves. Just to find a refreshing breeze, just to soothe her mind.

She made it down the path, gritting her teeth each time pain shot through her leg. She'd tried to stay off her ankle today, but during the peak lunch hours, she'd overdone it a bit. She'd pay for that come morning.

"Aunt Ana?"

She heard the soft voice, glanced up to find Laurel walking toward her. "Laurel, what are you doing out here all alone?"

"Don't tell Mom," Laurel said, her voice pleading. "I followed you down here."

"What is it, sweetie?"

"I...I wanted to apologize...for causing your accident."

"It wasn't your fault," Ana said, reaching out a

hand to the girl. "I should have been watching where I was going."

"But if I hadn't—"

"Laurel, that's all behind us now. And if you keep showing your mother and me that you can be trusted, she did say she'd let you go to the movies with Cal, provided you have an adult chaperone, of course."

"That's so lame."

"Yes, I suppose it does seem silly. But your mother loves you so much. She only wants to protect you."

"She doesn't care, really. If she did, she'd spend more time with us."

"She's going to do that, very soon."

"She never spent time with Daddy. And now he's gone."

Ana saw the pain and confusion in Laurel's big blue eyes. "Oh, honey, you can't blame your mother for that. Your father was sick, only we didn't know he was so sick."

"He died of a broken heart. I heard them—" Laurel stopped, clamped a hand over her mouth. "Don't tell Mom I said that."

"What did you hear?" Ana asked, though she was afraid to hear what Laurel had been holding so close. But they'd all been so intent on protecting each other, maybe it was time for a little honesty instead of the closemouthed civility that had colored the past few years between her sister and her.

"She said it had all been a big mistake. She accused him of loving someone else. But that's not true. My daddy loved my mother. I know he did. She was just never around to see that."

"Of course he did," Ana said, hoping Laurel hadn't heard all the truth. "But…it's not all your mother's fault. Your father worked long hours, too. They probably just needed some time together."

"They didn't want to be together. They worked to stay away from each other. And from us. They didn't even want us."

Ana tugged Laurel to an old washed-up tree stump near the dunes. Urging the girl to sit down, she said, "That's not true, Laurel. Your parents loved you. I don't care what you think you heard. You have to give your mother another chance."

"You sound just like Preacher Rock."

"Preacher Rock is a very wise man. You need to forgive your mother. She didn't cause your father's death. Neither did you. And she's grieving for him, same as you." Wanting to give the girl hope and honesty, she added, "You know, honey, sometimes grown-ups fight and say things they don't really mean and then they regret them for a very long time."

"Is that why she cries…at night?"

Ana felt the shock of that innocent question all the way through her system. "Yes, I guess so. I didn't realize she was still hurting so much."

"She isn't happy," Laurel said, her head down. "She was always so cool, you know, funny, and always taking us on these adventures before—even if it was just to the mall to shop and have an ice-cream soda. Even if she'd had to work late, she tried to make time for us. I miss that. I want my mom to be happy again."

"Well, you just contradicted yourself," Ana said. "So your mother didn't really neglect you or your sisters, did she?"

"Not really," Laurel admitted. "It just seemed as if she was always on the run, always busy. But she did try to make things up to us, and I know she's trying now. She neglected Daddy, though. That's why I'm so mad at her."

"You can't stay mad forever," Ana told the girl. "Trust me, I've tried that and it doesn't work."

Laurel sat there looking out at the waves. "I want her to be happy again, the way I remember them when I was younger."

Ana's heart went out to the girl. She'd seen so much in her short years—anger between her parents and now death. "Then, help to make her happy. You can't bring your father back, but you can forgive your mother for whatever you think

she did or didn't do for him while he was alive."
She reached out a hand to Laurel. "I can tell you
this, though, honey. Your mother cared about your
father. So please stop giving her such a hard time."

Laurel didn't answer right away. They sat in silence for a while. In that silence, Ana asked God
to help her family to heal.

"I'd better get back before she misses me,"
Laurel finally said. "You coming?"

"No, honey. I think I'll sit here a while. Tell
your mother not to wait up for me."

"Okay." Laurel started off, then turned, twisting her braid of hair as she hesitated. "Thanks,
Aunt Ana. You always know the right thing to
say."

"She sure does," Tara said from the shadow of
the trees just off the shore.

"Mom?"

"C'mon inside, baby," Tara said, her voice raw
with emotion. "I think it's time we had a long
talk."

Ana watched as Tara hugged Laurel close. Then,
hand in hand, the two headed back to the house.

Would her sister tell Laurel the truth? Ana knew
it would be hard for a teenager to understand, but
perhaps the truth was the best way.

The truth. Where was Rock? She finally had the
nerve to tell him the truth and he was nowhere to

be found. He'd disappeared during the mad rush
and she hadn't seen him since. Had all the commotion and confusion scared him away? She could
almost understand why. Today had certainly been
stressful and overwhelming, which might explain
why she felt like she needed a good, long cry. It
was just the letdown after all the excitement, she
told herself. Nothing to worry about.

And yet, she *was* worried. She was worried that
Rock had decided he couldn't be a part of all that
excitement and stress.

Ana sat for a while, and just when she was about
to give up, she saw him. He was walking up the
beach, carrying some sort of package. He wore a
white cotton shirt, the long sleeves rolled up to his
elbows, and khaki walking shorts. He was barefoot
and his dark hair was lifting out in the evening
wind.

Ana waved, then called out. "Hello there."

"Hello, yourself," he said as he made his way
up the shore to her, sand squishing against his feet.

She waited for a few measured breaths, then
said, "I missed you. Did you get my message? Are
you hungry?"

He came to stand over her, his head down, the
package held tightly in one hand. "So many questions."

Ana sensed immediately that something was wrong. "You don't have to answer my questions."

"Ah, but I owe you an answer. I owe you…so much, Ana."

"What do you mean by that?"

She didn't want him to answer that particular question. Suddenly, she knew what he meant. And her heart seemed to slip and scatter like a sand castle hit by a fierce wave.

"You left today," she said.

"Yes, I did."

"You left because you couldn't deal with what you saw. The people, the tea room, your mother. You still think I'll be like her, don't you."

"You are not, nor will you ever be, like my mother."

"But you came here tonight to tell me that you can't trust me, right? You can't trust yourself to have a future with me."

"'And in today already walks tomorrow,'" he quoted. "Samuel Taylor Coleridge."

Ana hauled herself up off the old log. "I don't need your philosophy, Rock." She swallowed, looked out at the glimmering waves. "I…need you. The real you."

"No, you don't need me at all." He let out a long sigh, pushed a hand through his scattered bangs. "I saw how happy you were today, Ana.

You were in your element. You have at last realized your dream."

"And you can't accept that?"

"I don't want to…jeopardize that."

She felt a slow burning fury inside her chest. "Well, too late. You put my heart in jeopardy the first time you kissed me."

"I was wrong. I thought we could just—"

"Just what, Rock? Share a stolen kiss here and there? Keep things sensible and sane? Stay in touch and be good friends? No commitments, no attachments, no strings?"

"There you go with too many questions again."

Ana faced him, her hair blowing in the wind, her eyes clouding with tears of frustration. "Well, get used to it. I intend to keep asking questions until I have some answers."

"There are no easy answers," he said, leaning close. "There is no easy solution, either."

She backed away, throwing up her hands. "You're right there. For years, I questioned why my sister had stolen my boyfriend away. Then I find out from her that he never really loved her the way he loved me. Now I feel like the guilty one. She is hurting right now, her children are hurting right now, because of some misguided sense of love her husband thought he felt for me. If I had talked to both of them, asked the right questions,

I could have told him that I stopped loving him long ago. I could have helped him find love with Tara again, the love they had to have felt when they first met and fell for each other.''

''It wouldn't have changed anything.''

''It might have,'' she said, glaring at him, hating the dejection in his words. ''And will it change the way you feel right now, Rock, if I'm completely honest with you?''

''I'd like a little honesty, yes.''

''Well, here's the truth. I love you. And...this morning, just before I came down to that waiting crowd, I realized that. I realized that a crowded room full of happy, laughing people can't replace a quiet room with the one person I love. I realized that having a restaurant and an art gallery can't replace a real family. I realized that at last I had everything I'd worked so hard for...and I still felt empty.''

She stopped, backed farther away at his attempt to touch her. ''I thought about you in your workshop. Thought about sitting in church, listening to your sweet, wonderful, quirky sermons. I thought about...what our children would look like. That's the truth, Rock. That's why I invited you back here tonight. I thought I could have it all, including you, but I guess that's not enough for you. You can't seem to let go of that image of the perfect wife you have planted in your brain. Well, I'm not perfect by a long shot, but I could have made you happy. I would have tried to make you happy.''

She turned away too quickly, her pride causing her to put too much pressure on her sore foot. She tried to make it up the sloping sand, slipped, groaned and waited to hit the ground.

But Rock was right there, catching her up in his arms.

''Ana,'' he said, her name a whisper in the wind. ''Ana.''

She looked up at him, tears flowing down her face. ''I could have made you happy,'' she repeated. ''I wanted to love you. I wanted us to be a family.''

''And I only want you to be happy,'' he said. ''Ana, please…''

''I'm going home now,'' she said as she pulled away.

''Won't you at least let me explain?''

''What's to explain? You can't get past your notion of what a carpenter's wife should be.''

''It's not that—''

''It's that and so much more. And I'm too tired and drained to deal with it tonight. I'm going home, to my house, to my tea room, to my life.''

''Take this,'' he said, his voice hoarse and raspy. He shoved the package at her. ''Just take it.''

Ana took the tattered, tissued bundle and hobbled her way up the path, tears causing her to stumble again. When she reached the porch, she turned to look out at the ocean.

And saw him still standing there, watching her home.

A week later, Ana finally got up the nerve to open the package from Rock. After a busy first week at the tea room, Tara and the girls had left for a long weekend in Savannah. Tara wanted to mend things with her children, starting with Laurel.

Ana had talked to Eloise almost every day, but hadn't seen Rock. When Eloise mentioned him, Ana simply said they had decided to be friends. She hadn't gone to church this morning either. She wasn't ready for that just yet.

Now that her ankle was completely healed, she'd taken to going on long evening walks on the beach. Since she didn't provide dinner unless it was a special occasion, most of her nights were free. And lonely.

Tonight, she stared down at the tattered bundle for the last time. Whatever gift Rock had wanted to give her, she would open it, then promptly return it. She wanted no part of a man too stubborn to see life staring him in the face. A man too stubborn to fight for the woman he loved.

She stood in her bedroom with the windows thrown open to the sea wind. She reached for the package and ripped the paper away, felt inside the bundle to pull out soft white flower-sprigged linen.

Ana gasped.

The design was old-fashioned but pretty, the blue flowers sprinkled across it reminding her of another such dress, which only reminded her of how much Rock had hurt her.

And yet, this dress beckoned her to forgive and forget. The neckline was a simple boat-cut, while the heavily gathered skirt flared from the waist into a sea of flowing tea-length folds. A huge cummerbund covered the fitted waist, its sashes falling down the sides to be tied in back.

"Oh," Ana said. "Oh, my."

She had to try it on.

She'd try it on, then send it back to him.

Hurriedly, Ana tossed off her t-shirt and shorts, then slipped the dress over her hips. With shaking fingers, she managed to get the zipper closed. With jittery hands, she managed to tie the wide crisp sashes into a bow at her back. It seemed to fit her perfectly.

Ana turned and looked at herself in the standing mirror. And at last, she saw that she was pretty.

Soon, tears were rolling down her cheeks.

"Such a sweet, incredible gift," she said, wishing she didn't talk to herself so much.

Angry, she didn't stop to think. She headed down the stairs, barefoot and still in the dress. She ran out onto the beach, her tears falling in earnest now. She was so angry at Rock Dempsey that she was going to march all the way to his cottage and just tell him how she felt. Ana walked and walked, all around the perimeter of the small island, moist sand clinging and then falling away from the crisp folds of her dress. Soon, she found herself not at Rock's house, but instead, standing in front of the Wedding Rock.

"I don't want to be *here*," she said, glancing around to see if anyone was watching her. She probably looked a bit demented, in her long white dress, her hair windswept and trailing around her neck and face.

I'm going home, she told herself. It would be a long, sobering walk, but it would clear her head— prevent her from doing something stupid like falling at Rock Dempsey's feet. She started out at a brisk pace, thinking about how she'd have to have the dress cleaned. Before she returned it to him.

Then she looked up and saw *him* standing on the other side of the big rock. Waiting for her. Blocking her way home.

"Ana," he said.

Ana enjoyed the way his breath seemed to halt with the word, and the way his gaze moved over her with a sweet intensity. Let him suffer.

"Hello, Rock. I was just coming to see you, but somehow I wound up here."

"In that dress?"

"Yes, in this dress. I suppose I owe you a thanks, at least. It's…lovely."

"Milly made it for me—for you, I mean."

"Milly did a great job, considering."

His gaze took in the gathered dress with wide-eyed appreciation, then returned to her face. "The design is from another time."

Ana lowered her head. "So are your notions regarding women."

"I have no notions regarding women. Ana—"

"Don't say it, Rock. Don't tell me you're doing this for me. You're doing this for yourself and you know it. Everyone on this island knows it."

"Yes, and I've heard it enough over the past week to believe that."

"Heard what?"

"Heard that I'm a mean, stubborn, ornery, old-fashioned, pigheaded man. Heard that I've lost the love of a good woman. Heard that I'm a fool and idiot all rolled up into one. I got enough glares in church this morning to make me seriously consider going on a long sabbatical. And I have to say, I'm mighty tired of the whole of Sunset Island telling me how to fix my love life. Even if they are right.''

Ignoring the ''even if they are right'' part, she said, ''I guess I could agree with all of that.''

''I don't want you to agree, Ana.'' He stomped toward her and then stopped, his hands at his side. Then he let out a groan. ''I want...I want you to marry me.''

Ana lifted her chin, her eyes locking with his. ''What did you say?''

Rock came up the path then, pulling her back to the rock and into his arms with a firm, determined grip. ''I said...I want you to marry me. Soon. And in this dress.''

''You're proposing to me, here in front of the Wedding Rock?''

''It's a good place to propose, don't you think?''

''What if I don't want to marry you?'' She did, of course, but she couldn't let him hurt her again.

''You do want to marry me,'' he said as he lowered his head, his mouth touching hers with the softness of moonlight hitting water. ''You do want to marry me. You love me, remember?''

''I also remember that you walked away from me and my tea room, and my art and all the baggage concerning you and your mother and who knows what else.''

''I came back,'' he said, his voice so low and

pleading that Ana instantly forgave him. "I came back, Ana, because I can live *with* all that a whole lot more than I can ever live *without* you."

"You...want me?"

"Of course I want you," he said on a shaky laugh. "With my every waking breath, I want you. I love you so much it hurts."

"I don't want you to hurt," she said, touching his face. "I want to make you happy."

"Then, marry me, here on the beach, in that dress."

"And I can keep my tea room?"

"You can keep *yourself*," he said. "I don't want you to change one hair for me."

"You can live with that?"

"I can live with whatever comes our way, because I love you. Can you live with me, in spite of my old-fashioned ideas, in spite of my love of a good home-cooked meal? In spite of me being me?"

"I love you being you," Ana said. "That's all I've ever wanted."

"Are you sure?"

"Very sure," she said. Then she reached up to pull his head down. Ana kissed him, sealing their reunion with a commitment from her heart.

And from above, the moon's light touched on the Wedding Rock, its gentle beams sealing God's commitment to Ana and Rock with a glistening, glowing blessing from the heavens.

Sunset Island Sentinel Society News— reported by Greta Epperson

One month from today, appropriately at sunset, Rock Dempsey will wed Ana Hanson on the beach in front of the Sunset Chapel. Sister of the bride, Tara Parnell, and her three daughters, Laurel, Marybeth and Amanda, will serve as attendants for the bride. Clay Dempsey will serve as best man for his brother. (And rumor has it that millionaire business tycoon Stone Dempsey might make a rare appearance at the happy occasion.)

A reception will follow at Ana's Tea Room and Art Gallery, to be hosted by Eloise Dempsey and Milly McPherson, with help from the entire tea room staff, and Ms. Dempsey's capable cooks Neda and Cy Wilson. (As many of you may know, Ana Hanson's tea room has become an island favorite, among both tourists and locals alike.)

Other tidbits about the upcoming nuptials: The bride will wear a dress the groom had especially made for her by none other than our own Milly McPherson. And Eloise was happy to share that the groom also gave the bride an antique diamond and filigree wedding ring that belonged to his wealthy, deceased grandmother, Eve Blanchard.

All in all, a happy love story. Another endearing detail regarding the couple—friends and family lovingly refer to the future bride as ''the carpenter's wife.'' But they also call Rock Dempsey ''the tea room lady's soon-to-be husband.'' This sure isn't going to be a traditional marriage, is it, folks?

Details to follow.

* * * * *

Look for brooding Stone's story,
HEART OF STONE,
coming in November 2003,
only from Love Inspired
and Lenora Worth!

Dear Reader,

Welcome to Sunset Island, Georgia. I love the ocean. Each spring I go to Gulf Shores, Alabama, with a group of friends I call the Surf Sisters. We spend a few days resting and walking along the beach, shopping, staying up late, eating chocolate and talking about our lives. This spring retreat renews our spirits and makes us appreciate the beauty of friendship.

While Sunset Island is from my imagination, the ocean is a true reminder of how beautiful God's world is. In this series about three brothers, I want to convey the message that God is truly our rock and our refuge, even when we've turned from Him. In this story, Rock and Ana both had mixed emotions about love and faith. Sometimes, what seems traditional and old-fashioned is really a step into the future—completely new and uncharted.

That's what taking a leap of faith can be—exciting, new, unexplored and hard to explain. And yet, taking that step brings us back full circle into a spiritual renewal of the traditional teachings of Christ.

I hope you enjoyed falling in love again with Rock and Ana. And I invite you to return to Sunset Island, when Rock's brother Stone Dempsey comes home to his brother's wedding and meets a woman who might just break down the walls he's built around his "Heart of Stone."

Until next time, may the angels watch over you—always.

Lenora Worth

HEAVEN
KNOWS

BY

JILLIAN
HART

John Corey's soul ached for his late wife but he tried
to move forward as best he could for their beloved
little girl's sake. Like a gift from God, drifter
Alexandra Sims wandered into their lives and
turned it around. Suddenly, John began to believe
in love again, but would Alexandra's painful secret
stand in the way of true happiness?

Don't miss

HEAVEN KNOWS

On sale June 2003

Available at your favorite retail outlet.

Visit us at www.steeplehill.com

LIHK

AN ACCIDENTAL HERO

BY

LOREE LOUGH

Book #1 in the *Accidental Blessings* miniseries

A head-on collision with burned-out rodeo star
Reid Alexander is the last thing Cammi Carlisle
needs! Pregnant, widowed and alone, Cammi is
returning to her family's Texas ranch in search of
forgiveness. Little does she know that the kind,
chivalrous man who just might be the answer to her
prayers is seeking *her* forgiveness....

Don't miss

AN ACCIDENTAL HERO

On sale July 2003

Available at your favorite retail outlet.